Roger Stephens

Minnows

197 Books
PO Box 65605
London N1P 1RS

First published in Great Britain in 2009
by 197 Books
PO Box 65605, London N1P 1RS

Copyright © Roger Stephens 2009
Cover artwork and design by Roger Stephens
Roger Stephens asserts the moral right to be identified as the author of this
work

A catalogue record for this book is available from the British Library

ISBN 978-0-9562995-0-5

for Lalage

post quam, ergo propter quam

contents

1969:

Another swing of the door
supersol bomb
'strange brew …
… girl, what's inside of you?'

`                          dusk`

civilian casualties
archive footage
fink's
in cold blood and good faith
stray shots
bearhug

1977:

`                  the bottom line`

inhuman resources
at six thirty-seven, precisely …
ancient greek
twirp
d.i.y.
wind up

'Yeah. I admit you're right. My suicide
note wasn't totally accurate. It wasn't
entirely your fault I killed myself.'
'Thanks. Any other words of comfort you'd
like to let slip?'
'Not just now. I'm feeling too wrecked.'
'Well, if you will insist on jumping.
Takes it out of you that way. You're lucky
to be still in one piece.'
'I am?'
'Yes, just about.'
'Pass me the mirror.'
'We don't have them here.'
'Oh,really. And where is here exactly?'
'That's for you to decide.'
'Oh,very Zen. Very Doors of Perception.
Looks like an exact replica of my room
actually. Down to the stain on the matting
from when the Exploding Galaxy were here.
They said it was something to do with the
lens for their light show breaking, but
I've always reckoned something much more
disgusting than that.'
    Across the basement kitchen table the
woman poured her husband a large scotch.
    'How long did you keep this up?' she
asked.
    'Until one of us chickened out.'
He gulped down some of the drink, spitting
the ice cube back.
    'The funny thing is I never dropped
acid, not once, and yet I usually held out
the longest. Same this time. I really,
really convinced Laurie that I really

7

*believed that I had killed myself. Weird.
He got quite freaked eventually and was
going to call the hospital. Time for me
to own up. . . . At which point he
claimed he'd only been kidding, the
bastard. Got a good mind to call him and
get my own back. What time is it in
Tokyo?'*

*'More to the point, what time is it in
Hackney? We've both got to get up
tomorrow.'*

'Any chance of a haircut?'

*'Of course. I've been suggesting it
for yonks.'*

*'Precisely how long is a yonk, exactly?
By the atomic clock? . . . Hang on I'll
get the flashing blades and the bib and
tucker. I want it really short.'*

'You don't mean now, surely?'
*He tossed a mane of silver shot black hair
as he got unsteadily to his feet clutching
the whisky bottle and attempted some
Jaggeresque gyrations. The kitchen chair
crashed sideways behind him. He began to
sing,*

'I can't get no-o hair reduction. . . .'

*'Not at one in the morning, love. I'm
too tired. Tomorrow.'*

'I can't get no-o direct action. . .'

*'I'm going to bed.' She made slowly for
the door, skirting warily round the one-
man rock band. The rock band lunged
towards her then went down on its knees,
one shoulder pulled free from the jacket
it was wearing.*

'Please, please, please. . . . don't
go.' The door slammed firmly shut.

He took another swig from the microphone
and then staggered to his feet, went over
to his briefcase on the sideboard and took
out his address book. Then he stumbled
back to the table, carrying the telephone
on a long trailing wire under one arm.

Half way across the room the phone rang
giving him such a start that he dropped
it. As it hit the floor the mouthpiece
came away from the handset and the top
came off the main part of the phone,
leaving the guts exposed. By some
electronic quirk the phone continued to
ring until he had managed to retrieve the
handset.

Then a voice he recognised said softly,
'Hurro. This is tomollow coring.'

1963

SHIT, SLOW . . . SHIT, SHIT SLOW

London, Christmas [1962]

'Shit, slow … shit, shit, slow,
  Shit, slow … shit, shit, slow.'
The bass player of the Thames Valley Stompers was trying to
crease the piano player without the trumpet player hearing. The
drummer was on another planet, as usual.

Ray, the piano player, had heard this witty variation once too
often to be amused and wasn't quite as ready as the bass player
to be fired for insubordination by old Eddie Calvert there. He'd
just got engaged, hadn't he? All right for some.

The bass player, Rick, edged closer. From the dance floor the
effect was that of a professional discussion of rhythm and
tempo.

'Don't look now, but I reckon the one in pink's the best bet
tonight. She looks like a goer to me all right.'

Ray played a couple more bars before turning his head in a
leisurely sweep of the hall, starting with an earnest scrutiny of
the rather attractive carving on the school organ. Without
pausing he took in the pink dress (not bad), and the spotty
herbert attached (quick head butt should do him), before
returning, after a cursory glance at the keyboard to make sure
that all was in order, to the musicology seminar.

'Yeah. All right, I suppose. Wouldn't kick her out of bed.'

The bass player's lip was curled ready for a distinctly
unscholarly rejoinder when he became aware that George had
launched into his favourite most sugary trumpet solo while
managing somehow to glare at them through the back of his
neck. Uncanny, that. Even the drummer had noticed, and was
almost keeping time.

The girl in pink, Jane, had suddenly had enough. She couldn't hear what John was saying to her, she hated the music and she was worried about what David was up to.

'Do you mind if we sit down for a while? I'm not too keen on the waltz.'

'No, not at all.' They slalomed through the handful of couples on the floor and found a seat.

'Two of the musicians were giving us funny looks, did you see?' Jane asked.

'What sort of funny looks?'

'Sort of randy-hostile. You know. Me randy, you hostile.'

'Perhaps I should have a word with them.' John sounded convinced that this would be a very bad idea.

'No, don't worry. I'll get David to sort things out if necessary. He is Official Boyfriend after all.'

'Yes, that's true.' John tried hard to sound pleased.

'And Your Official Academic Rival. Or rather Leader of the Opposition as he calls you.'

'Does he?' This was much better.

'Yes, often.'

The Sugartime Waltz ground to a halt to ragged applause, and the Head Boy announced the cold buffet. As the band trailed off the Deputy Head announced a spot prize.

'Can anyone provide me with a wooden cigarette lighter?'

There was a pause while girls searched their handbags for matches and then cheered as their boyfriends sprinted for the stage. The winner was immediately rewarded with a bottle of sparkling wine and then suspended for the duration of the imminent Christmas break for being under suspicion of smoking on school premises.

'Very witty,' said Jane.

'It's his annual joke. David tried to upstage him last year by strolling up with a bloody great cigar in his mouth doing a Churchill V-sign. ' 'We were not amused.' He got sent home.'

12

'So maybe he's planning some kind of revenge this year. What do you think he's up to?'

'Search me.'

'You're leaving too aren't you?'

'Yes. Oxbridge exams over at last. It's been a real drag. All the best people left in the summer. Just us swots alone and palely loitering. How about you?'

'I'm trying for Sussex. I want to do Sociology and that's the best place for it according to Roy. My adopted father.'

'Oh. I didn't know.'

'Yes, both my parents were killed, in Jerusalem, when I was little so Uncle Roy and Auntie Ada took me under their wing. Their left wing.'

'Yes. I know. David's always moaning about you going on all these CND marches.'

Jane looked up from a close examination of one of her stilettos.

'Oh, is he, indeed?'

'Yeah. You know.' John spread his arms out in crucifix pose. ' 'What a way to spend Easter'.'

'Very funny. … How about you? Quite happy with The Bomb?'

'Of course not. I know we could all die tomorrow, especially after Cuba. But I think that all this protest stuff is just teen-age rebellion.'

'Roy and Ada would be delighted to hear that. … So, what's your plan for world disarmament?'

John looked round the hall exactly as the piano player had done earlier. However this time his gaze was held by the moulded plaster on the ceiling and in particular what appeared to be a small trapdoor about forty feet above the stage. In all his five years of daily assemblies in this hall he had never noticed it before. Some sort of inspection hatch perhaps?

'You don't have to answer.'

13

John continued staring at the ceiling for a moment and then broke from his trance.

'Sorry. I was just distracted for a moment. … No. I don't really have a plan. It's just that I feel sometimes I'll have to disarm myself first.'

'How do you mean?'

'Oh, I don't know. Just something I've been feeling lately. I can't really explain. Forget it.'

There was a lengthy reflective pause and then John gave a start.

'My God! I've just remembered. The band is using the Sixth Form common room and I said I'd look after the refreshments. They'll be tearing the place apart by now. Will you be all right for fifteen minutes?'

'I'm not porcelain, you know.'

'OK. Sorry. See you in a moment. Unless you want to come with me.'

'What! Little me in the great big Sixth Form common room? With all those randy musicians?'

'Do you want to, or not?'

'What have I got to lose?'

***

In the common room the band were slumped in chairs, engaged in one of their favourite pastimes, arguing. The bass player was in the middle of a tirade that the others could have set to music, they were so familiar with it.

' … and I'm saying, George, that if we have to play any more Ted Heath numbers in the next set, that's me finished. Through. And I mean it this time.'

In his capacity as leader and paymaster the trumpet player wearily responded.

'Suit yourself, Ricky boy. You knew what the booking was. All round entertainment for the Christmas Dance. That's the booking and that's the set we've always done. Which does not mean rock around the clock. Or jazz around the clock, more's the pity.'

Recognising his cue the piano player came in.

'You and your bleeding Louis Armstrong. Ain't you never heard of any of the new stuff. I mean, Acker Bilk Mark Two. What's the point?'

'The point is, we, or rather I, get the bookings ...'

The other three supplied, rather raggedly, the traditional close to this particular number.

' ... and we get the peanuts.'

All passion, for the moment, spent there was a gloomy silence, broken eventually by a knock on the door and the entry of John and Jane carrying pints of beer and sandwiches.

At once there was a cheery 'I say, what-ho Jeeves' from the piano player.

The trumpet player gave him a withering glance.

'Don't pay any attention to him, son. Put it down over there. Thanks very much.'

Just loud enough for Jane to hear, the drummer muttered to the bass player,

'He's brought us some crumpet an' all!'

Jane went very pale and turned to John.

'Are you going to let him get away with that?'

John felt his knees give a little.

'I didn't quite catch what he said.'

Rick smiled at him.

'Perhaps I may be of assistance, young sir.' He ignored George's warning look.' My colleague, Bongo Bill here, appears to think that your young lady may be part of the light refreshments.'

Jane, still white faced, turned on her heel and, as she left the room, said to John,

'I'll wait for you back in the hall.'

As the door slammed behind her, John felt shame and relief in equal measure.

'Your bird's a bit stroppy ain't she, mate?' said Ray. 'Bit of a goer with it, shouldn't wonder.'

'She's not my girl friend, actually.'

'Oh, actually not?' queried Rick, affecting surprise.

'No. She goes out with someone in my form.'

As if John was Piggy in the Middle the conversation seemed to be flying back and forth just beyond his grasp.

'Oh, I see,' said Ray behind him, 'Quick knee-tremble while he's away, is that it?'

As John turned round, he felt a drop of the cold sweat of embarrassment run down from armpit to trouser band, like iced mercury.

He started to say, 'No, not at all …'

But it was too late. The ball had flown beyond his grasp and now it was with Rick, behind him again.

Rick was in no hurry, however. He waited until John had turned completely round.

' … or hardly ever,' he said slowly, underlining John's helplessness by lobbing the remark towards the drummer, who as usual was slightly out of synch.

'Wo'? Oh, yeah. Nice pair of knockers.'

John blushed furiously. In a desperate attempt to divert attention from himself he picked up the plate of sandwiches and handed them round in order of seniority. By the time the plate and last remaining sandwich had reached the drummer, it occurred to him that John was a little upset.

'Ta, mate,' he said sheepishly.' No offence, all right?'

'That's OK.'

There was a ruminative pause, and then John said,

'Actually, I wanted to ask you something.'

The trumpeter looked up warily,

'Fire away, squire.'

'Do you play requests?'

The piano player exchanged a swift conspiratorial glance with the bass player.

'Depends. There's one or two we do only at gunpoint. George here keeps a loaded revolver in his trumpet case to encourage us.'

George smiled despite himself. 'Keep it going, Ray. Might not even be peanuts tonight. Never know your luck.'

The piano player ignored him.

'Anything in mind?'

'I was wondering if you knew any Little Richard numbers?'

George had suddenly found something intricate to fiddle with in his trumpet case. It looked as though he would be busy with it a little while. Ray on the other hand was instantly transformed from desultory sandwich nibbler to chaired enthusiast.

'Not many! 'Tutti Frutti,' 'True Fine Mama', 'Can't Believe You Wanna Leave' …'

John took up the chant.

' … 'Ready Teddy', 'Baby', 'Slippin' and Slidin' ' … 'Here's Little Richard' . Side one. London Mono HA-C 2055.'

' 'Long Tall Sally',' from the bass player this time.

John pounced, feeling in total control now,

'That's track one on side two. And the recording engineer was Abe Robyn.'

The drummer pointed towards Ray and laughed jeeringly at him.

'Betcha didn't know that didja? Eh, Jerry Lee?' He turned back to John with just a hint of friendliness in his voice.

'So, how comes you know so much, then.'

'I like reading sleeve notes, collecting odd bits of information. It's just a hobby really.'

'Yeah. Like train spotting,' the piano player sneered, seemingly anxious to regain face by belittling John's knowledge.

There was an awkward silence and then Rick asked,

'So, which one do you want us to play?'

'My favourite is 'Good Golly Miss Molly.'

Rick looked at the piano player and the drummer.

'We could give it a go. Provided our great leader is in agreement.'

George's head emerged from within the jaws of his trumpet case and he gave a shuddering grimace, his eyes raised to the ceiling. 'No comment.'

John was still drunk on his own expertise.
'Actually, there are no trumpets on the original Speciality recording.'

'Is that a fact?' George sounded greatly relieved.

'Hard cheese, old top,' said Rick. 'You weren't needed anyway.'

Ray looked at John.' How fast do you want it?'

'Fast?' John looked puzzled. 'The same speed as the record, I suppose. I hadn't really thought about it.'

'Well, you better start. You're the singer.'

John's knees buckled.

'What! No. I thought … '

'There you go. Thinking.' Ray gently reproved him. 'You want to impress your bird, you gotta serenade her. Stands to reason.'

The others, even George, chimed in in agreement. Realising that he was outnumbered, John tried one last rearguard action. 'But I've never sung in public, only along to my Dansette, in my bedroom.'

To which there was a deafening chorus of,

18

'Opportunity Knocks.'

'Yeah,' said the bass player, you never know your luck. She might come across with the goods. Depending on how you do, that is.'

John felt himself starting to sweat again. He was back in the infants' playground again. A jeering circle of five-year-old toughs egged on by their girl friends throwing his brand new cap to each other above his head.

'Look, I've already told you …'

Ray had it now. 'Yeah, yeah, yeah. Girl of my best friend and all that. Suit yourself.'

Still bent over his trumpet case, George intervened,

'We're due back on stage soon, lads.'

'So, Mr Penniman, are you on?' John suddenly realised that Ray was trying to help him. However the momentum of his own embarrassment was hard to check.

'I'm not sure.'

'It's got to be yes or no.' Ray thought for a moment and glanced quickly at the drums and bass. 'Tell you what. As we hurt her feelings earlier on, we'll play it specially for her. How's that?'

'In that case … yes.'

Ray resumed his bantering tone, but this time it seemed to hurt less.

'See, I knew it. No smoke without fire. Dirty devil.'

Where there had been beetroot, John turned merely coral pink. Ray, noticing the improvement, patted him on the shoulder.

'Good. That's settled. Get a few pints down you, we call you near the end of our usual doings and Bob's your Auntie. What's your name by the way?'

***

About an hour later Jane and John were on the dance floor jigging about rather half-heartedly to one of The Stompers' original Thames Valley jazz numbers.

Every time John twirled round in an attempt to make his contribution to the dance less maypole-like it made him feel dizzy. He decided for a change to look up instead of round. As he did so he caught sight of the little trap door in the ceiling he had noticed earlier. He fixed on it, vaguely remembering something about ballet dancers doing it during their pirouettes. Just as he had completed his fifth fixed-gaze turn he saw the door slide half open, and part of a face he thought he recognised become visible. Then the door slid hastily shut again. As it did so dizziness overcame him and he staggered for a second with eyes closed in an attempt to regain his balance. Jane gave John a quizzical look.

'How much have you had to drink exactly?'

'Enough.'

'Enough for what?'

' 'Ah-ha!' said Piglet'. '

As he spoke the Stompers finished the number, and after the usual perfunctory applause, George stepped up to the mike, adopting his most toast-masterly tones.

'Thank you, ladies and gentlemen, for your overwhelming appreciation. To return the compliment, we would like to offer the opportunity for one of your number to serenade another of your number. So, ladies and gentlemen, instead of the last waltz would you please welcome the last straw, John Straw and … Jeezus Christ!'

While George was speaking, something from on high descended through the dark, until the spotlight caught, in Father Christmas outfit, sack and shiny leather boots and waving slowly to the startled crowd, a full sized human skeleton.

HEAVY PETTING

London, Spring

'So how did you manage to persuade Old Salami to write you such a good reference? After all the things he said to your parents.'

'Just told them you masterminded it all. ... No, seriously, I just said that I had been overwrought with exam pressures ... '

'Under wrought, more like.'

' ... and in a moment of youthful high spirits ... '

'Planned for weeks.'

'A week, maybe ... I allowed myself to commit an act of which I am now deeply ashamed. He was practically apologising to me by the end of it.'

John and David were queuing for their green card visas at the American Embassy in Grosvenor Square.

'How do you manage to tell such lies without blushing?'

'We're not all like you. No harm in a little power steering on the truth.'

'Sounds like yet another of your brand new traditional family sayings.'

'So?'

'I think it's immoral.'

The queue shuffled forward a few feet. David shrugged.

'Everything we do was immoral once, practically.'

'Or want to do. According to Jane, that is.'

Keeping his voice down to avoid being overheard by the other people in the queue, David hissed,

'What's she been saying, the lying bitch.'

'Just a bit of power steering.'

David raised his voice.

'What's she been saying? I want to know.'

The middle aged couple immediately behind suddenly began to discuss the weather, in such an exaggeratedly absorbed manner that John was convinced they were hanging on every word. He felt it would be a shame to disappoint them.

'W-e-e-ll, if you really want to know, she reckons the only reason you're going to the States is because she won't sleep with you.'

The discussion of barometric pressures increased in intensity.

'That's completely the wrong way round. She's been trying to stop me going by holding out on me. A bit like Lysistrata. Won't work. She likes it too much.'

Hot and cold fronts became, inevitably, the next item on the meteorological agenda.

'That's not what she told me.'

'Of course not. She's got her reputation at the tennis club to consider. She knows I don't want to be seen hanging round with someone like … what's her name … you know … always around … Gaping Gertie.'

With a gasp and a flurry of tutts and tsks the Met Office fell silent.

'Since I don't go to the club, I don't know who you're talking about.'

David put his arm round John's shoulder with a masterfully fake gesture of brotherly concern.

'You should, you should. Get some fresh air and ping-pong in your lungs. You'd clear up those spots in no time. No, I'm serious. You'll go blind thumbing through all those private parts and old records night after night. I mean, who cares what label Little Richard was on before Specialty. Why don't you do something? Learn to play an instrument, sing … anything.'

Behind them John could hear the beginnings of some rather half-hearted speculation as to the annual rainfall in Sumatra.

'That's pretty funny, considering you ruined my public debut with your Father Christmas stunt.'

'You'd probably have made a total prat of yourself.'

'Thanks very much.'

'That's OK. … The funny thing was, Jane was absolutely livid with me. Wouldn't let me get a finger up her for days. … Strange.'

As he struggled to make mildly interested noises, John's heart leapt.

***

Apart from the first Dylan album on the record player, Jane's bedroom was a shrine to the European rather than American counterculture. The decor was left bank bohemian with pictures of Juliette Greco and Jaques Brel on the wall next to the CND banner she had helped carry from Aldermaston last Easter. Although it was in her adoptive parents' house it was (apart from the lack of cooking facilities) a self contained bed-sit, and was respected as such by Roy and Ada, who almost never ventured in.

Jane and David were both sitting on the put-u-up bed, currently in sofa mode. Jane was smoking a Gitanes and occasionally knocking of the ash into a tray placed between them. David was slumped backwards examining the Dylan sleeve. Both their clothes were in the sort of disarray that indicated that they were taking an inter-round breather in the Garden Suburb Heavy Petting Championships.

'This guy can't sing for toffee.'

'He grows on you after a while. Some of the words are terrific.'

Jane went over to the player and turned up the volume on 'Talkin' New York'. They both listened for a while, until the line about ' … gotta cut somethin'.' Jane turned down the volume again and came back to the sofa.

'Great, aren't they?

'Yeah, terrific,' said David half-heartedly. 'He should go far … away.'

'Like you. I'm going to miss you terribly.'

'You singular, or you plural?'

'Don't be silly.'

David sat up and threw the record sleeve onto the floor.

'I'm not being silly. I hear you got quite quite matey at the dance. Telling him all sorts of things about us.'

Jane flicked her cigarette over the ashtray but nothing fell down.

'Such as?'

David stared at the floor with his elbows resting on his knees.

'Such as I'm only going to the States because you won't sleep with me.'

'Would you prefer the official version to be that I won't sleep with you because you're going?'

'I don't want any version, thanks very much. Official or unofficial. My private life's my own affair.'

Jane got up from the sofa and walked over to the window, then turned and leaned against the sill.

'And mine is everybody's?'

RECORDING NOW!

New York, Spring

Squeezed into the booth together, John and David had difficulty reading the instructions. After much clearing of throats and blowing of noses, money jingled in a slot and a panel with 'RECORDING NOW' lit up.

'Awopbopaloobopalopbamboom!'

Silence.

'Hello, everyone. That was John being spontaneous and nicking a line from his pop idol, Little Richard . . . . Talking of which, how's my idle pop. Only joking, Dad . . . . Well, here we are in America, and after only a week we're cutting our first record. Hope it sounds OK on your Dansette, Jane. Not as good as Mr Dylan, of course. He's waiting outside this very kiosk actually ... Over to John and the captain's log ... '

'What, er, oh ... Well, we had a very rough crossing, both sick for five days. Couldn't eat a thing. We almost got hit by a waterspout. Our average speed was only twenty-three knots instead of the usual twenty-seven, so we docked about a day and a half late. Last Friday in fact at seven minutes past twelve, Greenwich Mean Time ... '

'Thank you, the speaking clock. Yeah. As John said we had a pretty bad time on the boat, but we're OK now.'

John made seasick noises in the background. Both of them laughed hysterically for a while and then managed to control themselves.

'Sorry, folks, that was John, needless to say. These American milk shakes seem to have gone to his head ... oops ... there's a yellow light started flashing ... what's it say?'

'Thirty seconds remaining.'

'Already? Quick! Say something.'

'What?'

25

'Anything. Sing something. No, let me. I know. Finish as we started.'

David began singing, to the tune of 'Goodbye, Jimmy, Goodbye.'

'Goodbye, England, goodbye ...'

'Ruby Murray? Absolutely not.'

'Come on! ... 'Goodbye, England, Goodbye'.'

John joined in in deliberately discordant chorus.

' 'We'll see you again, but we don't know when, goodbye, England, goodbye.' '

That's it, folks ... Phew! ... Are we still ... '

The yellow light went out and there was the sound of some kind of braking mechanism. Another panel lit up. It read 'AWAIT RECORD AT EXTERIOR HATCH'.

With some difficulty, the two boys prised themselves free from the booth. As they did so, four very tough looking black youths took their place, not quite managing to close the door behind them. John and David exchanged astonished glances, not daring to say anything.

Through the crack in the door they heard a series of high-pitched screams, and then someone said,

'Ain't no acoustic in here, man. We gonna sound like Jackie Kennedy, man.'

A deeper voice replied,

'Watchoowong, man. We gonna move diss box over under duh subway or what?'

'How we gonna do that, man. You crazy?'

A light tenor voice lanced the disagreement with a splinter of song. The argument subsided and the voices took up the harmony, joined by the fourth member of the group. At the end of the chorus there was a short silence.

'Sound fine to me.' The door opened a fraction wider. 'What you think?' The lead singer had somehow managed to crane his neck out and was addressing John. David was trying to make himself invisible round the other side of the booth.

'I think you sound really smashing.'

There is a sullen silence within.

'Didn' I tell you. Even the honky don' like it.'

'No, I do. Really. It was great.'

The deepest voice spoke, slowly,

'That mean you gonna ring Pat Boone, tell him steal our song. Or maybe Elvis. Huh?'

The booth explodes with laughter and John feels his stomach unclench itself.

'Oh, no. I think that sort of thing is totally unfair. It's happened to Little Richard a couple of times now and I totally disapprove.'

'You tow-tally diss-aye-prove. Ain't that a great comfort to us all.' There was a hugely exaggerated chorus of 'Amens' and 'Hallelujahs' and another even louder burst of laughter, followed by the sound of a muffled discussion.

The lead singer's head re-emerged.

'Since you so tow-tally diss-aye-prove, me and the brothers was wondering if you'd like to make some voluntary contribution to our recording expenses.'

John said eagerly,

'Fifty cents? I would be delighted.'

'We wuz thinking maybe you could include some element of living expenses. By mutual agreement on inspection of your … wallet?

David had emerged from his hiding place.

'I think we should leg it.' he muttered. As he spoke there was a clunk in the exterior hatch as their record finally arrived.

John grabbed it and they both began running towards the subway. Instead of feet running after them they were pursued by yet more music.

They both couldn't help but stop and look round. The door of the booth was wide open and from it protruded, one above the other, four heads, four shoulders and eight beckoning arms.

' 'Oh, won't you stay, just a little bit longer,
won't you please, please, please,
say you're gonna'.'

***

Back at the run down hotel where they had a room, John chinned the top of the grocery bag as he fumbled the key into the lock. David tapped impatiently on the rim of the envelope containing their record. Sesame finally opened upon a monument to squalor, the inbuilt loathsomeness of the room enhanced by the chaos that two young men away from home for the first time had been able to create with effortless ease.

David slumped, seemingly exhausted by the weight of the record, onto the marshier end of the sofa. (He had decided that it was preferable to the lumpy regions, which were never the same size or shape two days running).

John dumped the brown paper bag on the part of the sideboard that even the cockroaches had begun avoiding.

' 'Stay' by Maurice Williams and the Zodiacs. Out on Top Rank in England. I wish I could remember the original label.'

He turned, frowning, towards David.' You don't really think they were going to rob us do you? Their music was far too good.'

'God. I can't believe how naive you are. Where on earth did you get the idea that musicians can't be thieves? Especially the blessed St Richard, of course?'

'I don't know. They just didn't look as though they were serious somehow.'

'Now you tell me.' David turned his head listlessly towards the cooker. 'So, what's it tonight then. Not tuna hash again, I hope.'

'You're quite at liberty to do the shopping yourself, you know.'

'I've told you, my shift finishes too late.'

'And you only get thirty seconds for lunch. Anyway, it's your turn to cook, I believe.'

'I've lost my appetite all of a sudden. I think I'll go out.'

'Suit yourself.'

John tore open the brown paper bag and, having selected them with his eyes shut, emptied the contents of the two nearest tins into a saucepan. It was only when they had begun to bubble and throw off the most unusual smell that he dared look. This was not a good idea. He didn't think he was ready for corned beef and condensed milk just yet.

'Where were you thinking of going?'

'Thought I might look at the Cafe Wha?. See who's playing.'

'Jay and the Americans,' said John automatically.

'Never heard of them.' David put his hands over his ears. 'No, don't tell me. I really couldn't give a shit what label they were on.'

John turned off the gas. He decided not to throw away his unlucky dip just yet. It was always possible that he had at last hit on a truly effective cockroach repellent.

'Mind if I come?'

There was a pause. David looked furtive.

'I thought I might go on my own for once. You don't mind, do you? We seem to be getting on each other's nerves a bit.'

John was astonished to find that his eyes were prickling with tears. Just like his mother. He turned away and began arranging the groceries in the kitchen cupboard.

'No, no … Go ahead. Me and the WMCA Good Guys'll have a quiet night in. If that should pall, there's 1010 WINS New York, Murray the K. . .

David sighed. This was just the martyred tone his mother used with his father sometimes.

'OK, if you put it like that, I'll stay.'

'No, seriously, you go. I'm feeling a bit washed out lugging cans of film all over the Bronx all day. I could do with the rest.'

'If you're quite sure.' David could have been his own father.

STIRRING IN THE UNDERWEAR

Los Angeles, Summer

In the canteen of the UCLA student Co-op supper had just
finished. John had drawn four hours washing up this week and
was just loading the last of the cups and saucers in the rack.

There were still a couple of people sitting talking at one of
the tables; that Negro girl with the peculiarly Oxbridge accent
and that scrawny bloke with a beard and knee-length khaki
trousers. Nigel his name was.

John couldn't make him out. No problem with the accent, it
sounded genuine Croydon, and all the business with the pipe
was suitably understated. (Luckily David was having to deal
with the ashtrays). It was just that he seemed so at ease with the
girl, as if she was his sister or something. But there was more
than that. She seemed to find him attractive …

'You silly twisted boy!'

It was Grytpype Thynne to the life, except half an octave
high. Good effort, Nigel. John turned round to see the girl had
pushed her chair away from the table and was leaning back
with her arms raised clear of the table. There was a mug on its
side in front of her, and David was mopping up a patch of
liquid just fast enough to stop it spilling onto her lap.

'I'm awfully sorry. I'll get you another one.' He turned and
called through the serving hatch to John. 'Any chance of
another cup of tea for Major Bloodnok here?'

'Grytpype Thynne, if you don't mind.' It was the girl. John
couldn't believe it.

As so often, Bluebottle came to the rescue.

'I will do it immediately, mein Kapitain.' John took a mug
from the tray he had been loading, rinsed it, filled it with tea
and took it through. As he arrived at the table, David was
saying,

31

'I don't believe it. A Goon Show fan club in California? You can't get the BBC out here, surely.'

Nigel shook another match to death and placed it in the ashtray.

'Unfortunately not. I managed to tape some off one of the local stations recently and I've been inflicting them on a select few ever since.'

John placed the mug of tea carefully in front of the girl, handle correctly oriented (assuming she was right handed).

'Here you are, mein Kapitain.' His Bluebottle impression had been the toast of the Remove.

Far from being impressed, the girl completely ignored him.

'Yes, that's right,' she said. 'I know them all by heart now. I can even tell whose voices they are. Harry Secombe, Peter Sellers …' She looked across to Nigel, frowning slightly. He took his pipe out of his mouth and was about to speak. She flurried a hand at him. 'No, don't tell me. Umm . . . Spike . . . Milligan. That's it.' She giggled delightedly. John pulled up a seat and sat down at the table. 'Not bad for a little black girl, lil' ol' Margaret from Macon, Georgia.' the girl said.

John felt his time had come.

'Macon, Georgia? Wow! You must know Little Richard.'

David made an exasperated face at the ceiling. Nigel sat back in his chair, clenching his pipe harder to conceal his amusement. Without looking at John, Margaret said,

'I must? I'd rather not. I don't care for all that screaming and wild talk.'

John was outraged. 'Screaming and wild talk? That's Rock'n'Roll. He is Rock'n'Roll. He knocks spots off all the white guys. I mean, Pat Boone doing 'Tutti Frutti'. Christ! Even Elvis … '

Margaret just had to look at him. 'Sounds like you're mighty keen on us black folks. We're all highly flattered, I'm sure. The only trouble is I don't think Rock'n'Roll is worth discussing. I stopped listening when I was old enough to stand on a chair and turn the radio off. It used to stop me concentrating on my reading.'

John tried desperately to regroup. 'Look, I'm not knocking reading. I mean I've just read this terrific book by James Baldwin … '

Margaret smiled. 'Another black faggot?' She exchanged an amused glance with Nigel. 'You trying to tell me something?'

John turned bright red, stood up from the table and ran from the room. David made as if to stop him but gave up.

In gently chiding tones Nigel said,

'That was a bit below the belt, Maggie. He was only trying to be friendly.'

'Maybe. But he was so patronising. Telling me to stick to my own culture, and not only that but which parts of my own culture to stick to. If I want to listen to the Goon Show and study Jane Austen, that's my business.'

'Jane Austen?' David sounded politely disbelieving. As he spoke his voice took on the suave tones of Grytpype Thynne.

Margaret took up the voice.

'Yes, I'm majoring in the nineteenth century novel, as a matter of fact.'

'I thought there was more than just the one.' David was rather pleased with the tone of rather silky superiority.

Margaret found her own 'amused' voice again.

'Very smart. OK, I'll rephrase that. I am currently perusing a number of works of fiction in the form of novels 'plural' written and published in the nineteenth century, with particular reference to those produced by Miss Jane Austen. Better now?'

David responded in the only way he knew how.

'Ying-tong-yiddle-i-po!'

***

33

In the three-bunk room that John and David shared with 'The Vegas Vampire' John was sitting at the communal desk examining the centrefold of Playboy magazine. On their winding three-month road trip, thumbing rides from New York to California, he and David had occasionally treated themselves to the latest issue out of the five dollars a day all-in budget each allowed himself. Breakfast sixty cents, lunch nought cents (they went without) and supper a dollar twenty-five. That left just enough to share the cost of the motel room in whichever town their last hitch had left them. With the aid of their sign 'London, England to … (next big town)' they had averaged three hundred miles a day.

He was still smarting from Margaret's remarks a couple of hours earlier. It was true that Giovanni's Room was about a homosexual relationship, but that didn't mean … What about the audience for some of Shakespeare's stuff. Were they all Hamlets, MacBeths, Lears? … He leaned forward to examine this month's Playmate more closely and felt a 'stirring in the underwear' as Ronnie McIntyre insisted on calling it.

There was a light tap on the door. John froze. The stirring ceased and began to recede. John could hear stifled giggles. There was another louder tapping noise. Whoever it was could hear the damned radio playing. John closed the magazine, and still holding it, got up and walked to the door.

'Who is it?'

'It is I, Blingebottle.' John recognised the voice of Judy, a canteen regular. With Sharon, presumably.

'And me, the famous Eccles.' Jolly well played, Sharon.

'What do you want?'

'Can we come in?'

'If you must.' John opened the door, holding the magazine casually in front of him in the unlikely event of renewed insurrection. The two girls came in, still suppressing giggles. Judy was rather large, her full dimensions camouflaged in a very loose-fitting dress. Sharon was much slighter, dressed in jeans and wearing impenetrably dark glasses.

Judy rushed over to John and, seizing his spare hand, held it out for Sharon's inspection.

'Big enough?'

Sharon raised her shades above her hairline and bent down to look.

'Yeah, plenty big enough.' The shades came down again.

John tossed his shield casually onto his bunk.

'Big enough for what?'

More convulsive giggles from Judy. Sharon was a little calmer.

'Judy wants you to do her a favour. Aye B-i-i-i-g Favour.'

Still unable to speak, Judy took his newly available other hand and led John over to the desk. There she slapped both hands down side by side. John left them there. Judy then made a span of one of her own hands and measured each of John's from wrist to tip. Having decided which was fractionally longer she measured it again, then placed her splayed fingers vertically against her own abdomen. With the tip of her little finger pressing on territory out of bounds to Playboy magazine, her thumb reached close to where John assumed her navel was.

'Eureka!' Judy shrieked. 'You're perfect.'

'Thanks very much. I'm glad to have been of assistance.'

'She means, you will be perfect,' said Sharon. 'For what she has in mind.'

Despite himself, John felt a faint stirring of interest and began to wish he had not thrown his reading matter quite so far away. He began to work out how he could manage to sit down and cross his legs with the right kind of swift casualness if the need arose.

'I'm sorry. I don't quite follow what all this is about.'

Sharon turned on Judy.

'Don't keep the man in suspense, Judy. Tell him.'

Judy collected herself, cleared her throat and spoke in a rather wobbly voice.

'Well, John, it's like this … er … How would you like … I mean how would you feel … '

More shrieks of laughter were triggered by this last word.

'Go on, Judy.'

'How would you feel … about … e r… ' The rest of the sentence was rapid fire. 'Puttingyourhandupmyskirt?'

John thought he might just as well sit down. Immediately. Anywhere. Oh, the floor. Fine. Might as well grab that old back number to rest on his lap in case he had to write anything down. Much better. More relaxed down here altogether.

The two girls, thinking it best to fall in with his Goonish ways, also sat down on the floor, crosslegged.

'Please don't take this the wrong way, Judy, but that's the last thing I would think of doing. I mean, is there any particular reason you want me to … if you want me to?'

'Oh, I do. I do.' Judy leaned forward earnestly.

'She really does, John.' Sharon's eagerness to convince him seemed even more desperate coming from someone who appeared to be blind. How could he refuse?

'But it's not what you think. Really. Not sexual, you know,' Judy went on.

'No, of course not. I didn't think … ' Was that a tiny shrug of disappointment from behind the Y-fronts? 'Erm … so … how can I help? What seems to be the problem?'

Judy took a deep breath,

'It's really crazy and stupid but … I was fitted for a cap …'

'You know, like a contraceptive Dutch cap?' Sharon was eager that John should have a complete understanding of the situation.

'… the other day . And I was practising with it this morning … '

'… inserting it properly, making sure it fitted over the cervix and all … '

'Do you want to tell this, Sharon? If you keep talking, maybe John can help you out instead of me.'

'Sawree.'

'So like I said, I was practising this morning and it's got stuck, and there's no one around with hands big enough to get it out. No one that wouldn't tell half the Co-op, I mean.'

'What makes you think I wouldn't?' said John.

'I know you wouldn't. I just know it.'

'You're the strong silent type. Trevor Howard, 'Brief Encounter,' right?' Additional dialogue by Sharon. John seemed to remember something about her being at film school.

'If I'm English I suppose I must be. A walking national stereotype, that's me.'

Judy whooped with joy. 'You'll do it? Oh, I just knew you would.' She began gathering the material of her dress in ample handfuls in preparation for pulling it over her head. Sharon stood up and readied herself to help her.

With by now no fear of immediate embarrassment, John stood quickly up.

'Hold it just a moment. I haven't quite made up my mind about this. I need a little time to think about it. There's no great rush is there?'

Both girls looked up at him with expressions of rapidly curdling gratitude.

Reluctantly Judy said, 'A couple of hours won't hurt, I guess.'

'Good, I'll let you know at the party. One way or the other.'

Looking slightly crestfallen, Judy and Sharon got up and left the room together in silence.

FINGERTIPS

Los Angeles, Summer

One of the impromptu parties for which the Co-op had become famous had caused the canteen to be transformed into a passing resemblance to Hawaii. Everyone had attempted some kind of fancy dress, even if it was only a flower behind the ear.

John and David were sitting on one of the long padded benches that lined the sides of the room, watching people attempting to cope with the tricky rhythms of 'Fingertips' from 'The New Ray Charles', Little Stevie Wonder. The harmonica breaks were particularly difficult to dance to.

'Especially if you're white,' John thought to himself. He noticed that Margaret, despite all her earlier protestations, was making a much better job of it than Jane Austen would have done.

David had to repeat his question.

'What made you rush off like that?'

'Just something that girl said.'

'Calling your idol a queer, you mean? Well, she could be right. I've always thought he was a bit suspect. I mean, 'Tootie Fruitie' … If the cap fits.'

'She doesn't know the first thing about him. As she said, she dropped all that in first grade.'

'Whenever that was. Any way, she told me to tell you she's very sorry she upset you.'

'Oh, did she?' John kicked himself for failing to sound completely uninterested.

'Yeah. We got talking after you left. About the nineteenth century novel and everything. Then later on, after we'd had a listen to some more of Nigel's tapes we sort of ended up in her room.' John could hear a familiar smug tone begin to creep into David's voice. It was the way their school had taught them to gloat over their achievements, their little victories over one another. She was very apologetic.'

'How nice for you.'

'Yeah, I really think it will be.'

'Will be.' So victory was still not seized although well within David's grasp. John was surprised to notice that he had stopped breathing, and took remedial action.

'So having dealt with 'Pride and Prejudice' it's still a matter of 'Persuasion'.'

David's tone became ever more matter of fact.

'Not too much persuasion, I shouldn't think. She really fancied me, I could tell.'

'Kept moaning and tearing her clothes off, you mean?'

'Oh no, much more subtle than that.'

'Wow! More subtle? Tell me more.'

'She kept folding her arms in front of her.'

The sheer anti-climax made John burst out laughing.

'Oh, well, in that case, you were home and dry. If that's the correct expression. How on earth did you manage to tear yourself away?'

'You've gotta be cool, man.'

'Fingertips' had finished and the scattering of people on the floor waited for the next record and possibly reinforcements.

'Forgive me for asking, but the folded arms thing is a new one on me.'

'It's a bit obvious isn't it?'

'Not really.'

David lowered his voice although the record was loud enough for him to have to shout. There followed the intricate dance of the hard of hearing, heads swinging to and fro as ears and mouths changed partners.

39

'It was to stop me seeing that her nipples were hardening with desire for me.' Swing.

'You really fancy yourself, don't you? Is that why you've been walking around with your legs crossed all afternoon. All that restless young blood' … Swing.

'OK, Grandpa. We know you've seen it all before. Or so you imply. Funny none of us ever met the girl.'

In mid swing, they both suddenly heard,

'Hey, you two English lovebirds. Why aren't you dancing?'

It was Margaret. She grabbed each of them by the hand and began to drag them onto the dance floor. John feigned reluctance at first but noticed that David appeared to be frozen in a half crouch, a look of fear and embarrassment on his face. In an unexpected spasm of loyalty to the old school tie, John decided that the best way to cover for David's little local difficulty was to follow Margaret onto the floor.

'What's the matter with David? Having a little trouble with his passion fruit?' Margaret asked innocently. John threw her a shocked glance, and seeing by her expression that she fully realised what she was saying, blushed furiously.

'You could say that.'

'Thank you, kind sir.' Margaret dropped him a mock curtsey in perfect time to the music. 'What else am I permitted to say? That he's cripplingly horny?'

John thought he might faint. It would serve to change the subject.

'That's something you'd have to ask him about.'

'Very right and proper. You don't want to break the locker-room vows of silence, do you?'

'I don't think it's my business, that's all.'

'And apart from keeping out of other people's business, what is your kind of business?' Margaret put her head to one side and gave him an appraising look, from head to toe and back again. 'No, let me guess. I think maybe you could be running that fruit stall . . . Now let's see. Are you Banana Bill, or maybe Pineapple Paul . . . or just perhaps . . . Queenie Quince?

John laughed. Margaret was being too outrageous to be embarrassing any more.

'Better ask my girl friend.'

Margaret's eyes grew round with surprise.

'You have a girl friend? We better stop dancing so close. The night has a thousand eyes. She could be anywhere.'

'Anywhere.'

'So, tell me, Mr Mystery Mango, who is she, where is she, the lucky girl?'

To give himself a break from shouting above the music, John put a finger to his lips and then across his throat.

Margaret clapped her hands and laughed.

'So loyal and so gallante. Are there no ends to this man's virtues, no beginnings to his vices?'

John kissed her on the neck.

'Try me,' he shouted.

Margaret put her hand to her heart in a gesture of shock and remorse straight out of silent movies.

'What about Her?' she mouthed.

John reinvented the talkies,

' 'Her' is far away.'

Margaret mimed great relief, wiping sweat from her brow, and then put her arms round his neck. 'If you say so…' she said into his ear.

They embraced in a slow dance among other couples dancing energetically to 'Killer Joe' by the Rocky Fellers. As the record ended Margaret smiled and, putting her lips to John's ear, sang very softly,

' 'Yes, we have a banana,

a great big banana today'.'

Then she kissed him long and hard on the mouth.

***

They were waiting for the next record to start, when John felt something cold splash against the back of his head and begin to trickle down his collar. He looked round to see David, with a half empty glass in his hand.

'Can't you find your own woman for a change. She's mine.'

Margaret said quietly,

'That's news to me, David.'

David laughed in disbelief, scanning the crowd for supporters as he spoke. 'After you've been giving me the glad eye all afternoon. I mean, come on.'

Margaret had an air of amused detachment.

'What is this? Disneyland?' She in turn shrugged at her supporters in the crowd, one or two of whom laughed.

David persevered, moved a step closer. John couldn't decide whether to restrain him or put an arm around Margaret. He decided to wait.

'What about all this?' David folded his arms tight across his chest and fluttered his eyes at Margaret. As he did so, a cascade of tropical fruit slithered down his left leg.

Margaret spread her hands in an appeal for an explanation from the other couples. They shrugged.

John felt compelled to speak.

'David reckons that folded arms are a sign of scarcely bridled lust. In a woman.' he added , to avoid any misunderstanding.

'Whaaaaat?' Margaret gave shocked yelp of laughter. One or two girls in the crowd joined in. Their male partners began to narrow their eyes like researchers who had stumbled on a new line of enquiry.

David turned to John.

'You keep out of this. You've done enough damage.'

Margaret's voice mingled amusement and indignation in equal parts.

'Damage? No, this is great. A whole new chapter for the Kinsey report. Hot news about the female psyche from a visiting English schoolboy.' She loaded the last word with sarcasm as she took a couple of steps towards David and confronted him with here arms tightly folded. 'So tell me, professor. Let me see if I've got the full gist of your thesis. Folded arms equal open legs. In a woman, that is.'

David took a step back and slowly unfolded his own arms.

'Look, can we drop this. It's getting a bit embarrassing.' He scanned the crowd with an unseeing, placatory grin. As he did so he fished out the last remaining fruit, a glace cherry, from his glass and gobbled it down.

Magnanimity in victory was obviously not on Margaret's agenda this evening.

'Oh, I see. So now we've got to stop because you're embarrassed.' A darting glance to poll the audience. About seventy five percent in her favour, it seemed. 'Listen, if you don't tell me what you've been saying about me, I'll start in with the tell tales that'll make you wish you'd settled for embarrassment.'

David clutched at a straw of playground defiance.

'Oh yeah? What sort of tales?'

'We could start with what really went on this afternoon.'

'According to you.' David had folded his arms again.

'It could end in tears. It looks like I've got a lot of support right now.' As they had been speaking girls in the crowd had been leaving their dance partners and now formed a tight circle round Margaret, John and David.

'How's the power steering,' John murmured from the side of his mouth.

'Fucked,' David's reply was equally furtive.

The outer ring of temporarily abandoned men was showing signs of restiveness, being largely out of earshot and unable to follow the conversation after 'That guy threw a Hula-Hula special at this other guy for dancing with that girl.'

Against a background of plaintive cries of, 'Put another record on, for Chrissake!' from the outer circle and stern hissing rebukes from the inner circle, Margaret began counting down from ten. When she had reached five, David spoke with a sigh.

'OK, fainites.' John smiled at this schoolboy relic. Margaret looked nonplussed. 'All I said was, it seemed to me as if you were trying to prevent your … er … bosoms from giving too much away.'

'Giving too much away? What are they, the Rockefeller Foundation?'

'No. I meant revealing your feelings.'

Margaret appealed to her supporters.

'Revealing my feelings? Now I'm a ventriloquist. 'Maggie and her Talking Tits.' She turned back to David. 'Now, look, David. I'm tired of all this stalling. Tell me exactly what you said about me, right now, or I'll have to start looking in the Yellow Pages under Lynch Mob.'

'I don't remember exactly.' The power steering was back in working order.

Margaret motioned towards John.

'Maybe your good ol' buddy can help out.' She turned to him. 'Well? Ready to save a friend by betraying a confidence?'

'If you put it like that,' John said doubtfully.

Margaret surveyed her posse. 'I think we do?'

There were nods and grunts of assent from those closest to her. John looked for confirmation from David, who gave a reluctant shrug of assent.

'What David actually said was,' the inner circle craned forward, the outer circle was hissed to near silence, 'he was sure you fancied him because you kept folding your arms in front of you, quote, 'to stop me seeing her nipples hardening with desire for me', unquote.'

John's last few words were lost in a burst of laughter, as some members of the posse collapsed on each other's shoulders. In answer to cries of 'Waddeesay? Waddeesay?' some girls still able to walk rejoined their partners and, complete with appropriate arm movements, explained what had happened.

The man in charge of the record player was emboldened to put on the Contours' 'Do You Love Me?'. Very loud.

As Margaret recovered from her hysteria, she dabbed her eyes and began dancing, on her own this time, but making it obvious that she wanted both John and David to join in. This they did, dancing in a loose triangle, dipping towards each other as they spoke or listened above the music.

Margaret spoke first to David.

'So you honestly believe that when you're with a girl, every move she makes is a silent tribute to your sex appeal?' Dip.

'Perhaps not every move. It's probably something Jane Austen tends to gloss over.'

Margaret slapped him gently on the cheek, and turned to John.

'Can you believe this guy?' Dip.

'Very rarely.'

***

'Do you love me?
 Do you love me?
 Do you love me?
 Do you love me?
 N-o-o-o-w that I can da-a-a-a-nce.'

David and Margaret had moved closer together and John was virtually on his own.

He was about to take a break on the bench when he was surrounded by swirling raffia and garlands of paper flowers, as

Judy and Sharon arrived and shared him wordlessly between them.

***

After a short while John began to tire of being a Hawaiian maypole and moved with his entourage closer to where David and Margaret were dancing. As he did so Margaret pulled away and the five of then formed a ragged circle for the rest of the record. David looked unhappy at this but did nothing. Margaret had been studying both girls and mouthed 'Her?' at John, as she caught his eye. John tapped the side of his nose in what he hoped would be an irritatingly arch fashion.

In the record gap Judy whispered to him,

'Well?'

'Fine thanks.' Why not irritate everyone while he was about it? Another record started.

Judy frowned, then pointed at her stomach and then at John. Margaret watched intrigued as John mimed putting on a surgeon's mask, taking care with the knot at the back of his head, and then rolled on a pair of invisible rubber gloves. Having done so, keeping his hands up in post-scrub position he headed for the door, with Judy and Sharon bobbing laughing in his wake.

David shouted near Margaret's ear, 'I never thought I'd see him go off with two women.' Swing.

'Afraid of losing your bet?' Swing.

'What bet.' Swing.

'First to lay in the U S of A?'

HOW WAS YOUR DAY?

'How was your day?'
'You tell me. You've heard it enough.'
'How can I when you never speak?'
'What is there to say about a job that no
longer exists?'
'You'll just have to make it up.'
'You wouldn't believe it.'
'I'd believe something.'
'What?'
'You weren't brain dead.'
'Thanks!' PAUSE
'So, how was your day?'
'I can't say. I can't imagine. I mean I
can't lie convincingly. I don't know what
would interest you.'
'Just words would do.'
'Any?'
'No. Just those which relate to the
question, 'How was your day?'
'True or false?'
'True or false.'
'You don't mind me lying to you?'
'We must unhinge the oyster, before we
test the pearl.'
'Taste?'
'Tee EEE ess tee.'
'Oh, sorry.'
PAUSE
'Well?'
'Yes, thanks.'
'WELL?'
'I did absolutely nothing. . . . Except
contemplate my navel.'
'What did you see.'

'A rather neat knot. A pucker of skin.
Bit like flesh disappearing down a
plughole.'
'Then what?'
'I poured salt into it. In case any
celery might happen along.'
'You don't like celery.'
'But if I did . . . '
'If.'
'. . . it would be handy. Wouldn't it?'
'So, with a navel-full of salt . . . you
just sat there?'
'For a while. Until one of the Bleaters
had trouble with the photocopier. Then I
stood up. . . after sealing off my navel
with masking tape. . .
'Naturally.'
'. . . and went over to view the carnage.
The Bleater had got its arm caught in the
machinery so that its face was down on the
plate and crisp copies of its flattened
features, like bafflement in a stocking
mask, were all over the floor.
    I ripped open my salt-cellar, sprinkled
a pinch on the cancel button and the
machine stopped dead. After pulling itself
free, the Bleater thanked me with tears in
its eyes and scurried out of the door.
'My hero!'
'It was nothing. . . . After that, 'to
encourage the others' I decided to paper
the walls with portraits of the artist as
a piece of involuntary software. One or
two may notice.'
PAUSE
'What's a Bleater, exactly.'

'Like a Punter, but even more woolly
minded.'
'Ah. . . . Then what happened?
'Nothing, for a while. Then I noticed
something funny was happening to my navel.
. . . You know that feeling you get at
the seaside when you're standing on sand
and the waves ebb round your feet and you
start feeling tottery?'
'Yes.'
'That's how my stomach started to feel.
Caving in from the outside. Must be the
salt. Corrosion, or something.'
'Has it stopped?'
'All but. Just a few trickles at the edge
of the crater.'
'Here, let me look . . . I can't see
anything.'
'Nor can I. It's just a feeling. You've
got to believe me.'
'Got to?'
'You'll leave me if you don't.'
'That's a bit heavy. (SINGS. TO THE TUNE
OF 'EVERY TIME WE SAY GOODBYE') 'Every
time I doubt your word, we die a little.'
Is that it?
'Not exactly. My word doesn't matter.
It's whether you believe in me or not.'
'If you give me enough to go on. Enough
about you. Enough about your day.'
'True or false?'
'Whatever.' PAUSE
'Pass the celery.'

TRILLS

Los Angeles, Summer

David rested on the handle of his shovel and looked across to where John was digging out the bank for the second garage. It was the morning after the Hawaiian party and David obviously had great news to impart. The problem was, how to steer the conversation round to it, particularly as there had not so far been any conversation this morning.

'So, how did it go last night?'

John kept on digging.

Grunt. 'Not bad.' Sigh. 'And you?'

'Smashing … Incredible really.' The shovel emptied itself onto the pile of earth twice more. 'So that's fifty dollars you owe me, I reckon.'

John leaned on his shovel.

'You'll have to prove it first. I want a blow by blow account.'

David was about to reply when their task-master emerged from the house. He was a tall rather twitchily hearty man in his mid forties called Dick, who appeared to have two aims in his dealings with them. The first was to get his money's worth from their labours and the second was to prevent them coming anywhere near his (much younger) wife.

Trill.

'Cup of char in ten minutes, my lads.' Dick also affected an 'English' accent. 'Time to rest then.' He trilled again and turned back into the house followed by David's unseen V-sign.

Both boys vented their fury on the clay for a few moments, until John said,

'You certainly don't look any different.'

'But I feel like a million dollars. Well, fifty, anyhow.'

David stretched out his palm. John hesitated.

'I'm going to need more detail.   I can't just take your word for it.'

'OK.   Provided you tell me what the three of you got up to last night.   You never know, you might get your fifty back, with interest.'

'Maybe.'

A few more silent shovelfuls.

David stopped and leant on his shovel handle once more.

'Go on then.'

'I asked first.'

'You promise to tell me afterwards?'

'Yes.'

'OK. … Well, we made it three times last night.'

'It?'

'Love.'

'How could you tell?'

'Tell what?'

'That it was love?'

David shrugged.

'What else do you want me to call it?'

'I want to hear what happened.   There's fifty dollars at stake remember.'

David sighed, exasperated.

'You're not cataloguing one of your bloody records now, you know.   However, if you insist on getting totally clinical, we had a screw, several screws. That's that.   And either you did the same at approximately the same time or one of us owes the other fifty dollars.'

John had not stopped digging.

'By screwing I assume you mean you got your cock into her and then came.'

'That's one way of putting it.   She also came, as a matter of fact. Moaning with joy she was.'

While the boys were talking, Shirley, Dick's wife, had emerged from the house, carrying a tray with tea and biscuits on it.   Dick hovered in the doorway, keeping a wary eye on them.   Shirley heard the last few words from David.

'Lucky girl!' she said.   John and David looked up and turned bright red. 'I've brought a spot of tiffin for you. We're fresh out of cucumber sandwiches, so I hope these cookies -sorry, biscuits- will do instead.'

'Oh, yes. Thanks very much,' said David.

'You boys are very welcome to use the pool when you next take a break,' Shirley went on. 'I imagine Dick will take pity on you in a couple of hours or so.'

From the house there came a nervous trill.

'Shirley! Leave the boys alone.   Let 'em enjoy their break. They've got another seven minutes.'

John muttered,

'Oh at least another seven.'

Shirley tried not to laugh then turned and shouted towards the house,

'Coming, master.' Then she muttered to the boys, 'Now there's a phrase you don't hear so often these days.' She turned and walked back to the house.   As she and Dick went indoors, David and John could hear the suppressed sound of bickering fading gradually away.

There was a thoughtful pause, and then David said,

'Christ, she's screaming for it.'

'You mean moaning, don't you? Can't say I've noticed any upheaval among the nipples.'

'OK. I was wrong that time. Nobody's perfect. But I'm telling you, that woman is asking for it.'

'It?'

'Not again. … A screw.   A good screw.'

'But no love making this time?'

'Maybe. I hardly know her.'

'You hardly know Margaret.'

'That's different.'

John frowned,

'How is it different?'

'If you don't know, I can't explain … In fact, if you don't know, I definitely win my fifty dollars.'

'How do you make that out?'

'Because, if you'd slept with either of those two girls you were with last night … '

'Sharon and Judy.'

'Yeah, Sharon and Judy. If you'd slept with them, you'd know what I was talking about. I wouldn't have to explain.'

'I slept with both of them.'

'Wow! You screwed two birds. In one night?'

'I didn't say that. I said I slept with them. After I'd helped Judy with her problem, we all fell asleep on the bed together.'

'And what was Judy's problem exactly?'

'She wanted me to help her get her Dutch cap out for her.'

David looked appalled.

'And you did?'

'After a bit of groping around, yes.'

David doubled up, clutching his stomach, as if about to be sick.

'Oh, God! How nause! How could you? In deliberate cold blood like that.'

'Nothing deliberate about you and Margaret then?'

'Making love to a woman and helping some stupid girl with her contraception problems are totally different things.'

John took another biscuit.

'I'm not so sure about that. It depends how you look at it. In both cases a male entered a female and then withdrew. In both cases the female expressed satisfaction, and the male was left feeling pretty pleased with himself.'

David took a lump of earth and shied it into the flowerbeds, startling the household cat, which darted to the edge of the swimming pool, did a right angle turn and then streaked indoors.

'You really are talking the most incredible crap, John. You're not seriously trying to suggest any similarity between me losing my virginity last night, and you fumbling about in the dark with a couple of overweight hula-hula girls.'

'You didn't fumble?'

'At first maybe, but I soon got inside.'

'So did I.'

'Only with your hand though. I'm talking about my cock. I got my cock inside Margaret. Then I came. That's how I lost my virginity.'

'And how did you feel?'

'What do you think? Great. Marvellous. Fantastic.'

'So it looks like we're quits.'

'Quits? But I've just said. There's no comparison. I had sex and you performed a rather warped act of charity. Where's the similarity?'

'Whether or not I've made love to anybody, I seem to have done pretty much the same things as you, only not quite in the same order. I went to bed with someone , or someones, I should say, entered the body of one of them …'

'Yeah, yeah, spare us the details.'

' … noticed that she was becoming excited by me … '

'Now he tells me.'

'… Made her come … and found that I was doing the same.'

'Outside her?'

'Yes.'

'You're still a virgin then.'

'Then she touched me.'

'Better.'

'Drew me towards her.'

'Warmer.'

'Put me inside her.'

'And?'

John tamped down the last of a little square of earth he had been smoothing during their conversation.

'I couldn't come. It was too soon after the last time.' John began striding up and down the ditch they were digging, like an American lawyer in front of a jury. 'So, members of the jury,' he said to the flowerbeds, 'on the night in question, did John Straw or did John Straw not lose his … VIRGINITY … or, to put it another way, was the whole greater than the sum of the events occurring to his (and her) private parts.'

'How do I know you're not making all this up?'

'You don't. Any more than I do.'

At that moment Shirley emerged from the house and walked towards them.

David had an idea,

'We'll have to ask her to decide.'

'You wouldn't dare!'

***

Dick looked up from the Wall Street Journal and glanced at his watch. She'd been gone three and a half minutes. What was keeping her? He got up and walked across the room and looked out. There was his wife watching intently as one of the two boy's -John, was it?- made the most strange gestures to her. He appeared to be explaining something to her. What was it? Some kind of crash course in car maintenance … dentistry? She was certainly finding the whole thing very amusing. Dick tiptoed to his desk draw and took out his old army binoculars. By the time he had focussed them, John had thrown his head back as if about to sneeze his head off. Instead off sneezing he collapsed into a smiling heap on the side of the trench.

David turned to Shirley,
'And I reckon he was still a virgin at that point.'
Shirley considered for a moment,
'I think we have a strong case for extreme heavy petting here.'
'Wait, there's more, 'John said.

Dick lowered the glasses slowly to his chest. Not since his army days had he witnessed such a parade of digital obscenity. Forefingers and thumbs circled and penetrated, limp and rampant in turn. And with each new configuration the three of them, not least his wife, laughed the more hysterically.

With a sudden decisive turn on his heel, he walked to the phone, and dialled a number.

'Hello? Elmore James? Dick Hassle here. I'd like you to act for me. I want a divorce.'

KING OF THE GOONS

Los Angeles, Summer

In the Co-op canteen John was preparing the communal pizza
for lunch. A few people were sitting round the tables chatting.
Margaret wandered in on her own and sat at a table.   She
opened a paperback she had with her and started to read. A
short while later Judy entered and, seeing John hard at work,
went over to speak to him. Margaret looked up, took amused
note, and looked down at her book once more.

Judy put her arm around John's waist.

'Hi! Need any help?'

John looked swiftly over his shoulder, saw who it was, and
started to pay very careful attention to his work.

'Oh, hello. No, it's all right, thanks.'

'Really, it's no bother.'

'Well, you could cut up a few of those mushrooms if you
want.'

His gesture towards them had elements of the flywhisk about
it.

'Sure.'

Judy relinquished her hold on him, picked up a knife and
took the mushrooms over to the sink to rinse them under the
tap. Having done that, and then dried them on a clean dish
cloth, she began to slice them up on that part of the chopping
board that John had not managed to imply was out of bounds.

When she had sliced up two mushrooms, she scooped them
up like snowflakes in her cupped hands and held them over the
section of the pizza that John had just finished working on.

'How do you want them? Scattered in handfuls or inlaid?'

John glanced across.

'I hadn't really thought.   Whatever you like.'

'OK.' Judy began leaking slices of mushroom from the widening gap between the heels of her palms as she moved her hands in a flattened zigzag a foot or so above the pastry and tomato paste. When her hands were empty she leaned against the table, facing John, and said,

'OK?'

John, still as absorbed as any watchmaker by the intricacy of his work, scarcely glanced at her.

'Smashing. Thanks.'

Judy began slicing up another mushroom.

'Do you mind me asking you something?'

John shot a furtive glance to see if anyone, especially Margaret, was listening.

'No, go ahead.'

'Did I really embarrass you that much the other night?' John grimaced in extreme concentration as he placed a piece of red pepper just so. 'Only, it's like you've been avoiding me for the last couple of days.'

Yes, Margaret was listening. He could tell by the very intense way she was examining the page in front of her.

'Oh, no. Not at all. I've just been a bit busy, that's all.'

'Rescuing another damsel in distress? You can tell me. I won't be jealous.'

Margaret was definitely smiling. David must have told her.

'Where's Sharon, by the way?'

'We're not Siamese twins. Any more than you and David are. Haven't seen too much of him lately either.'

'He's been a bit … er …'

'Busy?'

'Yes. In a way. … Look, I've got to get this pizza in the oven soon, or lunch will be late. We'd better get a move on, if you still want to help.'

Margaret decided that for the sake of appearances it was time to turn over the page. It didn't sound as though the two lovebirds were going to come up with anything amusing for the time being.

As she looked up, David came and sat down opposite her. John was heartened to see, through the back of his head, that there was every sign that they had had a row.

David reached half way across the table and began digging holes in the sugar with the spoon.

'Look, I've said I'm sorry. It was just a spur of the moment thing. A joke. We wanted to settle the bet and she happened to be handy to appeal to.'

Margaret looked slowly up from her much-scanned page.

'I'm quite sure you did appeal to her. I just object to having my private life dissected in minute detail in front of a total stranger. A white stranger at that. … How would you feel if I did something like that? Just drove down to Watts, picked the first brother off the streets at random and told him all about you. For a fifty dollar bet? I mean, it's so cheap.'

'It was a joke.' David sounded exasperated.

'Who's laughing? As far as I'm concerned, you and I are finished.'

'Come on.' David stopped stirring the sugar and stretched over to touch Margaret's arm. She shrugged him off.

'No, I won't come on. Just because we've spent a couple of nights together doesn't mean you own me, white boy.'

David began stabbing the tabletop with his fore finger to collect the scattered grains of sugar there.

'I never said I did. I just thought you felt the same as I do … about you.' He licked the end of his finger and began stabbing again.

'That depends very much on what it is that you reckon you feel.'

'Surely you know. I'm crazy about you.'

Margaret nodded.

'You're crazy all right. King of the Goons.' She closed her book.' Look, I've got some work to do. Maybe I'll see you later, after I've had a chance to cool off.' Margaret stood up and walked away from the table. David stayed sitting for a moment, drawing invisible patterns between the microscopic dots of sugar on the tabletop. Having completed this task to his satisfaction he dusted his hands off, and then as an afterthought bent forward and blew the tabletop clean.

**

In the kitchen, Judy and John were putting the finishing touches to a magnificent tray of pizza. David wandered in and reached out to steal a fragment of the decoration. Judy slapped his hand away.
'Don't pick. It took ages to arrange those olives.'
'What's up with Margaret?' asked John. He tried very hard to sound off-hand.
'Oh, nothing. Just something about the way we settled our bet. She didn't like the publicity.'
Judy looked up from the olive she was slicing.
'Bet? … Publicity? What's he talking about.'
'Oh, nothing,' John said.
In a voice heavy with resigned disbelief Judy said,
'If you say so.' And continued slicing.
'Any luck with the Thunderbird?' John asked.
'Yeah, I reckon.'
Judy put down her knife.
'Now this I gotta hear. This ain't no way nothing.'
David scooped up some pieces of olive unopposed.
'Just some distant relatives. They've got a white open top and said I could borrow it one evening. I thought this evening would be as good a time as any.'
'What about Margaret?' asked John.

'What about Margaret?' David answered through a mouthful of olive.

'Washing her hair, do you reckon?'

'Could be.'

'You guys have that in England too?' Judy's tone was amused and sympathetic.

'You bet,' said David, as he pulled open the oven door and pushed the pizza tray inside. After closing the door again he took off his apron and hung it up behind the kitchen door.' So, where do we start?'

'Well, daddy-oh,' said David. 'I thought we'd play it this way. Catch the last wave at Malibu, the biggest burger at Howard Johnson's and then …who knows?'

'Dragging main for the action?' Judy asked.

'If you say so,' said David uncertainly. He turned to John. 'What's she on about?'

'Driving up and down the town's principal thoroughfare on the qui vive.'

'With the radio on,' Judy added.

'With the wireless attuned to the frequency of one's choice.'

David raised an eyebrow at Judy.

'He thinks he's poking fun at himself, but he's not. He always talks like this. Quite spontaneously.'

'Yeah, he's real cute.' Judy hugged John tight, until he put an embarrassed arm round her shoulders and then let it drop.

***

On the Malibu sand the Thunderbird was parked with its doors open. The radio was playing the Beach Boys 'Surfin' USA'. John, David and Judy were lying in a row sunbathing. Judy was singing along to the record.

'This record is boss. They come from round here. One of my cousins used to date Al Jardine.'

'They're all right, if you like that sort of thing.'

David groaned.

'Here we go. Another sermon on the mount. More evil white boys stealing from the poor old negroes.'

'It happens to be true,' John said.' That record is based on 'Sweet Little Sixteen' by Chuck Berry.'

Judy lolled her head in his direction.

'My big brothers used to listen to him. I thought he was dead. You never hear from him.'

John rolled over and rested his head on one elbow.

'No, mainly because he's been in jail for the last few years. For taking a minor across a state line. The fact that she was a white girl made it worse.'

'Worse for the girl?' Judy asked.

'For him. They came down on him like a ton of bricks. Put him in prison. While he's in there these people steal one of his songs, change all the words and have a hit with it. And then, to make matters worse, his own record company bring out an album of some old tracks, complete with totally phoney sounding crowd noises and have the nerve to call it 'Chuck Berry Live on Stage . . . featuring Surfin' USA'. Which turned out to be our old friend 'Sweet Little Sixteen,' featuring the original lyrics.'

'This is all fascinating,' said Judy, 'but what does it matter now? You've got to make progress.'

'Yes, but not by arrant plagiarism.'

' Arrant plagiarism!' Judy turned to David. 'Can you translate for me, please?'

'He means stealing.'

DOUBLE DATE

Los Angeles, Summer

Margaret was in her room at the Co-op, working at her thesis in rather a distracted fashion. Having grown tired of the view from her window, and having completed an extremely elaborate doodle on the words Pride and Prejudice, she went over to the radio which had hitherto been tinkling away in the corner, like some undernourished harpsichord, and tuned it to the most raucous station she could find.

'You are tuned to WBX Seventy Seventy in Down Town LA. We rocket to the future, but we don't forget the past. And talking of Golden Oldies, Little Richard is in town. Yes, the 'Tutti Frutti' man is playing Hall of Fame Night at Rockin' Jay's in Watts. You better be there, you better believe it. Shake a tail feather with the Reverend Little Richard Penniman. God God-ah-Mighty ... '

'Good Golly Miss Molly' started playing. Margaret struggled to concentrate for a while, then threw down her pen and put her head in her hands, a finger of each tapping in time to the record.

***

Back at Malibu, Judy stared at David aghast and amused.
'And you told this woman everything?'
'We had to. To settle the bet.'
'No wonder Margaret was upset.'
John couldn't stifle his own curiosity.
'And you're not?'
'Oh no. It was just friendly with us. No big deal.'
David shut one eye and lined up his big toe with the distant figure of John, who was still out there body surfing. He threw a pebble at the toe and missed.
'Listen, Margaret's no big deal.'

'You kidding? You're crazy for her. A girl can tell. You don't have to be cool with me.'

David gathered a handful of smaller pebbles and as he spoke threw them in a steady succession at his toes, which were lined up like so many coconuts at a fair ground shy.

'I don't know if I'm crazy about her.' Miss. 'I just think about her all the time.' Miss. 'I don't even know if I like her.' Hit. … Miss. 'I just want her. I thought once we'd been to bed, that would be it.' Miss. 'Collect wild oats certificate, and off home to Blighty and student life among the redbricks. Assuming one of them will let me in on the strength of my A-levels and the Head's efforts to perjure himself on my behalf. 'Hit. … Hit. 'Ouch! . . It doesn't seem worth it now. England seems unreal, as much a dream as America used to be.'

Judy laughed.

'Man, you got it baaad! But look on the bright side. So has she. I betcha.'

David dumped the remaining pebbles on the sand.

'You really think so? It's crazy. We've been like that.' He pressed his palms together. 'For two days, and yet I can't tell what she's thinking at all.'

'Maybe she's confused too.' Judy mused for a moment. 'Why not ask her for a date tonight?'

'Ask her for a date? You make me sound like a teenager.'

'You are a teenager, aren't you. And so is she, just.'

'I don't know what good it will do.'

'You'll maybe have fun. That's what good it will do. Believe me, she'll take one look at your T-bird and all will be forgiven. It's an old Californian tradition.'

David sighed.

'We could try, I suppose.'

'Attaboy! … John and I'll come along to lighten the mood. You know, double date?

'Another old tradition?'

'You learn fast, limey!'

***

The dresses were down to a short list of three, with the green silk a definite maybe, so it was just a matter of the hair now. Suddenly Margaret's radio became bigger than the room. She looked out of the window to see this big white coupe blaring at her. Who was that in the white tux with the single red rose in a crystal box? She bit her lip in joyful panic. It was David, come to ask her for a date.

' … despite having gone too far already, and with a car full of gooseberries.'

'Your grasp of American tradition, combined with your old world charm have quite persuaded me. I would be delighted.'

David escorted Margaret to her side of the car and then climbed behind the wheel.

'Where to, gang?'

'How about a little cruise while we make up our minds?' said John.

'Yeah, why not,' said Judy. 'Unless there's something you have in mind, Margaret.'

'I do, as a matter of fact. As we're hell bent on recapturing our early teens, let's go see what's shaking at Rockin' Jay's. We could be in for a treat. You especially, John.'

***

Pinned to a door in a sleazy row of shops, a hand written notice read,

'Tonite - The 'Original' Little Richard and his Band -'Ooh My Soul'.'

Beside the notice lounged a large youth in shades, surrounded by a clutch of small boys of similar though less menacing appearance. The 'teenagers' stared at each other with mingled apprehension and disbelief.

Shades strolled towards the car, followed at a respectful distance by his entourage.

'Hey sister, what's happenin'.'

'We're going to the show. And I'm not your sister.'

'Suit yourself, Betty Mae. Shades turned his attention to David. 'You park here, that'll be twenny dollars 'tendance fee.'

'No thanks. It's quite all right. We can manage.'

'Don't you unnerstan' English? Ah-tenn-dance fee, thir-ty bucks. You dig?'

'It was twenty just now,' David retorted.

'That's inflation, man.' Shades laughed briefly, and was echoed by a ripple of sawn-off mirth from his understudies. 'So, what's it gonna be? Forty for the attendance now, or a thousand for the respray later?'

'More inflation?' David said as cheerfully as he could manage.

'Yeah, and the tyres too maybe,' said Shades. 'If we got time.'

'That's no problem,' said Margaret. 'You'll have plenty. We're with Little Richard, so when we come out with him after the show, this Bird better be new. Else he gonna get upset, and his attendants gonna give you a whole lotta time - recovery time, you dig?'

Shades took half a step back from the car and raised his hands in mock surrender.

'OK, sister. Just puttin' you on a little. Tell these dudes they got safe passage. Lucky for them we in a beneficial frame of mind, talkin' with the foxy lady.'

THE ORIGINAL

Los Angeles, Summer

Rockin' Jay's had once been a small cinema. The front stalls had been removed to form a makeshift dance floor. The place was perhaps two thirds full, with twenty or so people dancing to records played by the DJ/MC.

As the sound of 'Fingertips' faded, the lights went down and a spotlight played on the faded pink stage curtain, there was the crackle of jack plug in amp and snick of drumstick against cymbal. The audience shushed itself to a giggly semi silence.

'And now, ladies and gentlemen, please give a big hand to the one , the only ... Mr 'Tutti Frutti' ... Mr 'Long Tall Sally' ... Mr 'Baby Face' himself ... Mr Undisputed King of Rock'n'Roll ... The Original ... Mr Little Richard!'

The curtain pulled raggedly apart to reveal guitar drums and bass players and a battered looking piano, which was as yet unattended. The band staggered into the intro to 'Good Golly Miss Molly'. The spotlight played stage left. Offstage someone was singing the first lines to the song. Suddenly he emerged, holding a hand mike on a long cable and sang his way across the stage, to take his seat at the piano just in time for the instrumental break. The dance floor had filled now and couples were doing the Watusi and shaking a tail feather with a vengeance.

Judy grabbed John's hand to drag him onto the floor, but he hung back, staring at the stage in angry bewilderment.

London, Summer

At the same time in England, it was late afternoon. Jane and
her 'parents,' Roy and Ada, had arrived back from a camping
holiday and were unloading the car. Jane unlocked the door
and pushed through the small snowdrift of mail on the doormat.
She fell on her knees and scrabbled in the pile until she found
what she was looking for.   Jane held it to herself for a moment
then, without turning round, passed it behind her to Ada, her
eyes screwed up tight.
   'You look, Ada, I can't bear to open it.'
   'You are a funny girl.   There's nothing to worry about.   I'm
sure you've passed.'
   'Please.   I just can't.   My hands are trembling.'
   Ada opened the envelope with deliberate speed and unfolded
the piece of paper inside.
   ' English - B, History -B, French -C.   You've got 'em.   Well
done, darling.'
   Roy, who had just come in with the suitcases, joined them in
the celebratory huddle.
   'I can't believe it,' said Jane.   'A B for History.   I was sure
I'd failed.'
   'Nonsense,' said Roy.   'I told you so.'
   He moved the cases out of the way and then went to retrieve
the other letters.
   'Looks like your lucky day.   There's one here from the
States, post marked Los Angeles.'
   'It must be from David,' said Jane slowly.   'I don't believe it.
It must be the first one he's written, apart from a couple of
cards to his Mum and Dad.' She opened the letter as carefully
as Ada had done her exam results and began to read.   Her eye
darted about the page looking for the bad news she felt sure
was there.   Gradually the fragments began to make sense.

'Crazy about her … hope you will understand one day… her name is Margaret … I wanted to let you know first … her name is Margaret … I've decided to stay on here for a while… times we've had … haven't told John yet … Margaret … I have let you down, but I cannot help myself … I wanted Margaret … hardest letter in my life … ' Jane collapsed on the first steps of the staircase but couldn't cry. Another huddle formed, this time in sorrow.

Los Angeles, Summer

Meanwhile back at Rockin' Jay's it was near the climax of the set. The floor was packed and all but one of the audience was having a very good time. The sole exception was John, sitting on his own in the centre of the middle row of the stalls. Margaret tore herself away from the beat and came over to shout in his ear.

'Anything the matter? You should be dancing like crazy. I thought Little Richard was your hero.'

'Sure. I'm not so happy with the 'Original' Little Richard though.'

'I don't get you.'

'I'll explain later.'

A song ended and members of the audience shouted out requests. John suddenly got up and pushed himself through the crowd to the front of the stage.

Standing directly below the microphone John cupped his hands round his mouth and bellowed,

'Long Tall Sally!'

A long look, then,

'Where you bin, man. We already played that.'

'You left out half the words.'

69

'What you saying, man.' A wide-eyed appeal to his group and the audience. 'I don't know ma own songs?'

'It would seem so.'

'It would seem so?' This dude sure ain't from Macon, Georgia. He ain't even from LA. Where you from?'

'London … England.'

'London, England? How 'bout this guy. He come from London, England and tell me, Little Richard, how to sing ma own song. The sweat of my brow' A disbelieving shake of the head to the audience. 'Tell you what, London , England. I bear you no grudge. The King of Rock'n'Roll has no false pride. You say I left out some lyrics, I say you put them back in again, London, England.'

He reached down towards John as if to help him up on stage. John hesitated a fraction, as if checking for low flying skeletons, and then clambered up. The crowd applauded wildly.

As he stood up, the singer put his hand over the microphone and whispered,

'You better not be kiddin' me, London.'

Then, louder, to the crowd, he shouted,

'The British are comin', the British are comin'. Ooh, mah soul, Good God Ah-mighty.'

Then he leapt to the piano and began to pound out the intro to the song.

***

House side of the curtain the audience began to disintegrate into little knots of friends and drift towards the exits.

Stage side it was much more business like, with the drum kit half dismantled and the amplifiers dead.

John walked slowly down the corridor with the star of the show.

'You know what, England? You sing pretty good for a white boy. Like a born again Little Richard.'

John blushed at the compliment, and dared a little joke.

'I was just going to say the same about you.'

There was a long icy silence.

'Time you and me had a little talk, brother.' They were walking down a corridor which had a false ceiling composed of pipes for water and heating but probably not music, and had arrived at a couple of doors. One was marked 'Band' and the other one 'Singer'. This room was not much larger than the cabin John and David had suffered in across the Atlantic.

The door closed behind them.

'OK, London, what's your problem? You try lean on Little Richard, you the one got problems. Ain't nobody gonna take from the Original.'

'I'm not trying to take anything. I just want to see fair play.'

There was a tap on the door.

'Who's there?'

'Some guys reckon they're friends of yours,' a voice said.

Thought the door, John heard Margaret say,

'John, are you in there?'

'Yes,' he whispered. He turned to the 'Original'. 'I think it would be best if you let them in.'

A mutter. 'This better be good, Fair Play.' Louder.' OK. Let 'em in.'

The door swung slowly open.

'Judy, David and Margaret,' said John with a sweep of his hand. 'Please meet the 'Original' Little Richard.'

Margaret stepped forward with her hand outstretched.

'From Macon, Georgia, right?'

'Thassright, sister. The Georgia Peach hisself.'

'Which part of town?'

'The wrong side of the tracks, where the poor coloured folks live. Yonder by the baptist church.'

71

'On Arlington and Duke?'

There was a moment's hesitation.

'Arlington and Duke? Sure thing.   Ain't been back in quite a while.   Bin a lot of changes.'

'Including moving Arlington five blocks parallel to Duke? At least, that's how I left it.'

'Five blocks? Sure thing.   Like I said, it's been a while.'

John said, very casually,

'Maybe you can remember Abe Robyn a little better.'

'No I don't remember ever living there.'

'Well that's something I suppose.' John made a superhuman effort not to burst out laughing. 'Abe Robyn was the recording engineer on most of your hit records. Maybe you were never introduced.'

There was a very long silence.

'So, the 'Original' ain't the Greatest.   You gonna turn me over to the lynch mob?'

Sensing that John was at a loss for words, David said,

'No need for that.   If you can do us a little favour in return, your secret's safe with us.'

***

Outside the club, the audience had dispersed leaving just a little knot of people standing round the Thunderbird. Shades and his followers were becoming impatient.

'They ain't gonna show,' said one small replica. 'They out the back way. We oughta start a little panel beating, maybe.' He looked eagerly at Shades for confirmation.'

'We give it thirty seconds,' said Shades with the ghost of a nod.   'Then we start.'

The group began looking round for useful implements as one of them started a countdown.

'… five… four… three… two… '

The doors of the club swung opened and the King of Rock'n'Roll emerged, surrounded by his courtiers.

Shades stilled the countdown,

'Well, Good Golly Miss Molly, if it ain't Little Richard hisself.' He made a mock bow, then straightened and jerked his thumb towards the T-Bird. 'This your car?'

'You oughta know better'n that. Little Richard don't own nothing but a brand new Cadillac.'

Shades and company began to look triumphant and menacing, scenting blood. Margaret, Judy and John exchanged worried glances and David opened his mouth, about to say something. 'How - e - ver … he ain't too proud to accept a ride with his friends, even if they only got a poor old T-Bird.'

'You sure these your friends?' Shades sounded very disappointed.

'As sure as Arlington meets Duke in good ol' Macon, Georgia.'

They climbed into the car and David started the engine. As they drove off Shades tried to regain some face.

'Hey, man! What about the thirty dollars? For watching the car?'

The Original looked around at the others and then turned to Shades.

'We just decided. We feeling generous, so we ain't gonna charge you nothin'. '

FRAT RATS

Los Angeles, Summer

David had been driving for a full two and a half blocks before anyone spoke. They had been too busy enjoying the breeze and the view and the admiring glances from people waiting for the WALK sign at the crossroads.

The 'Original' leaned forwards from the back seat to where Margaret was sitting next to David.

'Hey, sister. What's happenin'?'

Margaret turned round to him.

'What's happening right now is, we're on a double date. What's happening next I've absolutely no idea.'

'I think maybe there's a party somewhere in the Co-op tonight,' said Judy. She turned to The 'Original'. 'You wanna come. What's your name by the way?'

'You can call me Otis,' said The 'Original' and smiled a smile to out-dazzle the Real Thing. John was amused to notice that the pencil moustache favoured by Little Richard was in this case just that, drawn on with eyebrow pencil and now smudged and barely visible in parts.

'OK, Otis,' Judy resumed. 'Do you wanna come to the party? If we can find out where it is, that is.'

'Why, thank you Miss Scarlett.' Otis leaned forward again to tap Margaret on the shoulder. 'You hear that, honey. They done invite us poor coloured folks to their party.'

Before Margaret could reply, David said,

'She's inviting you too. She lives there. With all of us.'

Otis gasped with exaggerated amazement, putting on hand over his heart.

'With all of you?' he squeaked. 'How many you got?'

'Not including overnight guests, there's thirty three altogether,' said John.

'Ooh, mah soul,' said Otis wonderingly. 'This Co-op sure sounds like a place for a party. Sounds like it is a party.'

Otis laughed heartily and slapped a thigh, which turned out to be John's. He let his hand remain there briefly before returning it to his lap. John made a show of putting his arm round Judy's shoulders, which made her shoot him a surprised, pleased glance and snuggle up to him. Out of the corner of his eye John saw Otis give a 'win some, lose some' shrug.

By way of making conversation, John asked,

'What about your band? Don't you think you ought to tell them where you are?'

Otis appeared to go into shock.

'Tell them? Listen, those guys think I'm the Real Thing and there ain't no way I want to disappoint them.' He paused, 'Besides, I can't afford to pay them.'

'Oh, I see,' said John uncertainly.

'Yeah, travelling expenses been getting a little heavy lately.' Otis laughed to himself. 'Yeah, you could say that. I been travelling to some very weird, expensive places.' Otis drew air through his nose in a long continuous stream, held his breath a moment and let it out all in a rush. He looked around the car for a reaction, saw none and then laughed aloud, slapping a different thigh from before, his own this time.

***

As the car drew up outside the Co-op canteen, John could see a knot of people standing in the open doorway. Although the light was behind them he could make out the unmistakable stoop of Nigel and the dark glint of Sharon's sunglasses behind him. Two or three of the larger male Co-op members who appeared to be forming a tense protective barricade in front of her. As they climbed out of the car and were recognised the group relaxed. Nigel turned round to Sharon and said,

'It's all right, it's only a few Goons. Nothing to fear.'

John mistook this for a cue for a funny voice. He chose
Bluebottle, but when Nigel didn't reply in character (of an
evening he usually favoured Minnie Bannister) or even smile,
John realised that something was wrong.

So did Otis. There was no sign of a party let alone thirty-
three passports to depravity. However he contented himself
with an injured glance at Margaret.

'Nothing to fear?' asked David. 'What's up. Where's the
party?'

Judy had broken through the loosely knit cordon and was
talking to Sharon. They whispered together for a moment and
then the two of them walked back into the canteen and sat
down on adjoining armchairs together.

Nigel pulled his tartan dressing gown round himself and took
a spit crackling drag on his extinct pipe. He was shivering
slightly.

'The party, to coin a phrase, is over for the time being, but we
were awaiting further developments.'

'How do you mean?' asked Margaret, who had come up the
steps and was standing by him. Otis, John and David had
followed and stood close behind.

'Perhaps I should have said 'awaiting further visitors',' Nigel
went on.

'Gatecrashers you mean?' asked David. 'They'll be a bit
late.'

'Not for what they want,' said Nigel.

'What's that?' asked Margaret.

'Revenge.'

'The food wasn't that bad was it,' said John. He spoke in his
own voice this time.

Again Nigel didn't laugh. Something was definitely up. In
the awkward silence that followed Judy rejoined the group.
Behind her John could see Sharon slumped back in her chair,
dabbing under the edges of her sunglasses with a handkerchief.

'She seems pretty upset,' Judy said. 'I can't get her to tell me what happened exactly, or who was responsible.'

'It was definitely not a Co-op member,' said Nigel. 'There were a couple of Frat Rats hanging round trying to gatecrash earlier on, and we think it was probably one of them. She couldn't see who it was in the dark but she didn't recognise his voice. As she came running back in here he called out that they'd come over and smash the place up if she told us what had happened. Which she has, kind of.' Nigel did laugh now, very briefly. 'Hence the vigilante group.'

'How many Rats do you think they can muster?' asked Margaret.

'Twenty, thirty, maybe,' said Nigel.

'We should be able to match that.'

'Yes, but have you seen the size of some of those guys? They're all sports jocks, Basketball … Football … '

'Sounds mighty tasty,' murmured Otis. 'Reckon I'll stick around.'

John looked at him in amazement.

'You don't have to you know. You're quite free to go. This isn't your quarrel, after all.'

'Maybe not, but I want a piece of the action. Thirty white boys stomping all over me. Wow! Wouldn't miss it.'

Margaret turned on him.

'Let's get this straight. We're here to protect Sharon from further assault, not to give you a treat.'

Nigel took another draw on his still unlit and empty pipe.

'There might be a way round this that makes everyone happy.'

'Including Sharon?' said Judy quietly.

'I'm sure she would approve anything which avoided further bloodshed,' said Nigel. 'And once we've seen off the immediate threat we can take the matter further with the proper authorities.'

'So, what's you're idea?' asked Margaret.

Nigel took his pipe out of his mouth and knocked the bowl against the palm of his hand. A few threads of tobacco fell out and he stuffed them back in.

He turned to Otis,

'With you permission, and given you're expressed penchant for a bit of sporting rough and tumble … '

Otis grinned hugely,

'You're speaking my language, man.'

'… I would like to suggest that we appoint you our Champion to engage with the appointed Champion of the other side and do battle until honour is satisfied. You should get a damned good hiding for your trouble, which, from what you say, you would find rather to your liking. There is an ancient tradition behind such encounters which should satisfy even the most Neanderthal members of the Fraternity, naming itself as it does after the usual clutch of letters from the Ancient Greek alphabet.'

As Nigel spoke they could hear the approaching sound of male voices chanting in unison. As it grew nearer it became possible to distinguish the names of just such a quartet of Greek letters as Nigel had described.

'Kappa, Delta, Sigma, Tau,
  Nothing's gonna stop us now!'

The chanting was accompanied by the clashing together of what sounded like beer cans.

A couple of minutes later a dozen or so large crew-cut youths in tee shirts and Bermuda shorts had gathered by the low perimeter wall at the foot of the path leading up to the canteen. The clashing of cans fell silent as one of their number stepped forward.

'You gonna hand that bitch over, or we gotta come and get her?'

Nigel eased his pipe into his pocket, took a faltering step forward, and cleared his throat nervously.

'Gentlemen, we have an alternative suggestion to make. That we settle this matter by unarmed single combat, according to the ancient traditions, between the champion fighters proposed by each side. The winner to take no further action.'

The Rat spokesman looked Nigel contemptuously up and down, his gaze lingering on the wrinkled pyjama bottoms visible below his dressing gown.

'You must be the Champion. You're already dressed for hospital.'

The other Rats found this highly amusing. Nigel waited for their merriment to subside and then said,

'No. We've chosen someone else who's raring to go.' He motioned Otis to move forward into the light from the canteen windows.

Otis, who was still in his stage clothes stood at the top of the steps, hands on hips.

'Hi, y'all,' he called out. 'Which one of you boys is man enough for me?' He walked slowly down the steps towards the chief Rat. When he was within touching distance of him, Otis put up his fists in a grotesque parody of the bare-knuckle style.

His opponent gazed at him blankly for a few seconds, and then turned to face his colleagues. He said, addressing one of the group in particular.

'You better sort this out yourself.'

The other replied,

'I ain't messing with no nigger faggot.'

Almost unnoticed during these events, Sharon had come forward to the doorway and was standing next to Nigel, observing this interchange.

'That's him,' she whispered. 'The guy the first guy's talking to. He did it.' She was pointing to the largest and most belligerent looking member of the group.

'You're absolutely sure about that?' Nigel whispered back.

'I recognise his voice.'

'Yes, it is rather distinctive.'

Nigel made his way down the steps past where Otis was standing, and stopped within a few feet of the reluctant warriors.

'Gentlemen, since you have not seen fit to take up the gauntlet thrown down at your feet, I claim victory by default. I trust you are in agreement.' Nigel received no sign of acknowledgement . 'In which case, we merely ask that the culprit makes a full confession and apology. We will then consider the matter closed.'

The two Rats continued to ignore Nigel. They didn't speak or move a muscle for several seconds, then the Chief turned to the Culprit and said,

'Did somebody fart?'

Nigel persisted,

'So you won't apologise?'

The Culprit looked at Nigel for a moment and then said,

'This guy wants his asshole for a necktie.'

'Very well then,' Nigel persisted 'You leave us with no alternative but to contact the authorities.'

'Kiss my ass, Dagwood,' said the Chief Rat, and he bent over, pulling down his shorts and indicating with a stabbing finger the area in question.

'Yeah, me too,' said the Culprit and did likewise.

At this all the other members of the visiting team followed suit, as if performing some well rehearsed football play. Within seconds the perimeter wall was topped by a row of fleshy moons.

There was a moment's dead silence followed by the squeal of car brakes. John looked up, half expecting to see a couple of police cars emptying out in their direction.   Instead he recognised three very angry faces that he had last seen oozing musicianly cool behind the 'Original' a few hours ago.

With scarcely a glance at the human coconut shy they walked swiftly up to Otis and, grabbing him by his arms and legs began carrying him bodily down the path again towards their car.

Otis made no attempt to struggle, reserving his energies for a high volume mixture of beseechment and abuse. His abductors responded in low monotone, reserving their strength for some later top to toe treatment they had in store for him. John could only judge what they had said by the way Otis's invective veered between two extremes.

'Hey easy now, you dumb motherfuckers. You drop me and you smash your future, you hear?' (Angry mumble from abductors) ... 'You got it all wrong, they kidnap me those white dudes.' ... (Louder, angrier mumble) ... 'Took all the money I was saving for you.' (Menacing or perhaps outraged silence) ... 'OK, OK , Just gimme time, I got a deal going down.' (Burst of cynical laughter) ... 'They was planning to lynch me.' This last pronouncement was followed by a chorus of 'Good!' from his bearers.

Meanwhile the moons were one by one experiencing total eclipse as their governing planets became drawn into the wake of this cosmic disturbance.

By the time Otis was being stuffed into the back seat a crowd of very large, very fit not altogether sober people had surrounded the car.

The Co-op people followed and edged their way through until they were standing close to back door of the car. When Otis saw them, he shouted to Margaret,

'Hey, sister. You gotta help me. These guys is serious. They gonna turn the corner, then they gonna turn me inside out.'

'I thought that's what you like.'

'Hey now, we ain't talking heavy petting with a bunch of college kids. These guys are real disappointed.'

81

The Chief Rat stepped forward and looked through the window into the car.

'You planning on going somewhere?' he asked the driver. 'We haven't finished with this guy, so maybe you'd better let him out.'

The driver became indignant.

'This cat owes us money for the gig tonight and we ain't got paid.'

'I told you,' said Otis indignantly. 'These guys took all the money, after they kidnap me.'

'We didn't,' said Margaret flatly to the two band members flanking Otis in the back seat. 'Why are you telling these lies about us?' she said to Otis.

'Oh, I didn't mean you, sister,' said Otis with all the ingratiation he could muster. 'These white guys, you know?'

'No, I don't,' said Margaret even more flatly. She continued, 'How much money does he owe you?'

The driver hesitated a moment.

'Hundred and fifty dollars.'

'And you'd let him go for that?'

The driver looked out at the crowd surrounding the car.

'In the circumstances, sure.'

Margaret turned to the Chief Rat.

'You reckon you can raise that?'

He looked staggered.

'You want us to pay this guy's debts? Are you out of your mind?'

Margaret was icily calm,

'Perhaps you'd all prefer to face charges of gross public indecency. Not to mention the little matter of raping one of the girls here.' In the background could be heard the sound of a police siren coming their way. 'So what do we tell them? Very sorry, officer, false alarm, or…?' Margaret paused, waiting for a reply.

Very reluctantly Chief Rat turned to the rest of the group and said,

'OK, guys, that'll be a voluntary contribution of ten dollars a head.' He began collecting the money in the front of his tee shirt, which he had pulled out and doubled over to form a kind of pouch. When at last the required sum had been reached he handed it over to the driver, who nodded to the others to let Otis go. As he got out the door slammed and the car started, then shot off down the road, scattering the people who had been standing in front of it and almost colliding with the approaching police car. This made the police car do an immediate U turn and set off in hot pursuit.

Everyone watched open mouthed until the two vehicles had disappeared from sight.

Everyone that is but one. The one who sat on the top step weeping and the sound of whose weeping made everyone turn their heads. It was Sharon.

AHOVE

Delayed information can be like a time bomb. Memories can be events. She remembered that he had called her by a special name in his language. Nearly twenty years ago. He had said it in a special way, and explained the words were only used to express extreme love.

'Ahove shellee,' is how these words had sounded to her. But she didn't know how they looked in Hebrew. She didn't know what they meant in Hebrew, except that they were special. Because he said so, twenty years ago. Even though he had gone and she didn't know if she would care for him again, she cared for having been loved like that, and kept the words within her as something to hold onto sometimes, when she had been low. They had a mystery, deliberately fostered by her because she had never asked any of the many Israelis she had met since then what they meant.

She was afraid to because they may have mistranslated, or said the words differently, or laughed at her for having made something special of an everyday banality. She wondered how she herself would have broken it to a foreigner that he had been bolstering his own self-esteem by making a talisman of some English commonplace.

CAMERA OBSCURA

Bristol, Winter

'Oh, won't you staaaaay
Just a little bit longer?'
As John walked in the jukebox in the students' union coffee
bar was going strong.

He had arranged with Jane to meet here but there was no
sign of her. He bought a coffee and sat down at a table near
some particularly rowdy students, two of whom, judging by the
way that the girl had her face buried in the bloke's shoulder,
were anxious to demonstrate that they knew each other fairly
well.

Despite his disapproval of the way all these English groups
were ruining the American originals, John found that his feet
were tapping.

On his way from the bus station he had noticed that the
leading offenders, The Beatles, were playing at the Colston
Hall that evening.

'Please, please, please,
Say that you're gonna.'
The Hollies they were called. Their record was much faster,
without that strangely leisured pleading that Maurice Williams
put into the song. He wondered what had happened to the
group that he and David had run into that time in New York at
the recording booth. Their version would have been better than
this.

'Hello, John.'
He looked up to see Jane standing in front of him, completely
transformed. Her hair was up from its Shetland pony fringe,
and she was wearing black boots and a shiny plastic mac.

'Hello, 'he said. 'I didn't recognise you.'

Jane sat down opposite, perched on the front edge of the armchair.

'Do you want to stay here?' she asked. 'I thought we could go for a walk around town a bit, as it's such a nice day.'

'OK.' John gulped down the last of his coffee froth and they both got up.

'No luggage?' asked Jane.

John rummaged in the pocket of his donkey jacket and pulled out a toothbrush, still in its wrapper.

'Only this,' he said.

'I thought we could go up by the suspension bridge. It's quieter there.'

'OK,' said John again.

'Don't sound so enthusiastic,' Jane said.

They walked in silence for a while then said together

'Have you heard from him at all?'

They laughed at the clash and then John said, with a mock bow,

'After you.'

'Nothing since the letter,' said Jane with the bright tone that often denotes pent up tears. 'The one where he said he wasn't coming back.'

'He told you why.' John's intonation hovered between question and statement.

'Only that he'd been shagging this girl and reckoned he was in love with her.'

'He didn't say that did he?' John sounded unambiguously shocked.

'No, of course not. Not to me. I just thought I'd translate for you.'

'How do you mean?'

'Into blokespeak. Isn't that how you all talk to each other?'

Jane sounded even more light-hearted as she adopted a fruity growl. Only the stiffening of her upper lip gave her away.

'Pulled this fantastic bird last night, gave her a really good shagging.'

The small bus queue that they were passing got the full force of these last three shouted words and saw too how Jane burst into tears and started running up the road away from John. He had no option but to run after her away from their as yet silent disapproval. He was saved from the possibility of pursuit and citizen's arrest by a particularly spry looking brace of geriatrics by the arrival of the long awaited bus. The two old women had to content themselves with shouting.

'You best leave her alone, young man,' and

'That poor girl.'

As the bus pulled slowly past them on the slight gradient at the turn of the corner into Victoria Square, John caught up with Jane, who had by now slowed to a fast walk. He fell in with her pace and they walked in silence until they were within sight of the bridge.

'Is that really all you went over there for,' Jane asked. 'To lose your virginity? I would have thought a quick visit to Soho would have been cheaper. And much quicker.'

'Not all,' John said. 'We did have a sort of jokey little bet with each other about who'd be first. But it wasn't at all serious.'

'And he won, in a light-hearted sort of way.'

'Well no, actually.'

'Oh?'

'It was a sort of dead heat.'

'How did you manage that? … No, I don't want to hear. It must have been absolutely disgusting.' Jane shivered and pulled her shiny coat tighter round her. After a moment she nodded towards a small building on a hill overlooking the bridge. 'We could have a look at the camera obscura if you like.'

'OK'

***

At the top of some stairs they entered a dimly lit room, in which they could make out a handful of people leaning on a low rail and looking down onto a grayish white disc. On the surface of the disc small figures moved against a background that was alien and yet familiar. After a while John realised that he was watching an animated and peripherally distorted watercolour of the park that he and Jane had just walked through. Above the disc was a periscope-like device with which to scan other parts of the field of view. As you turned it this way and that it spurted more watery images onto the white.

John watched fascinated as a man the size of his thumb picked up an invisible stick and threw it for his dog to fetch, and again as two finger high boys kicked an unseen ball about between two trees. He had an overpowering urge to reach out and peel them from the surface of their tiny world, but satisfied himself with stretching his hands out beneath the watercolour spout and watching the by now de-focussed blobs skim across the surface of his palms.

'Don't interfere with the mechanism, please.'

The voice came from an attendant sitting almost invisible in the gloom to one side of the chamber.

John pulled his hand quickly back.

'Naughty boy!' whispered Jane approvingly and patted him very gently on the wrist.

The chamber was beginning to fill up now and John felt the urge to cause further public unrest by attempting some shadow animals or doing his famous impression of a U-boat commander. He was sure it would make Jane laugh.

'Perhaps we ought to go,' he said, after a short hesitation.

'OK,' said Jane, sounding disappointed.

They left the chamber, and shortly afterwards became part of the entertainment for those who had stayed behind. The small boy in temporary charge of the periscope tracked them until,

88

small but horribly deformed, they walked off the edge of the world.

As they did so, a battered transit van drew up beside them and an emaciated looking youth leaned across from the driver's seat and rolled down the window.

'You students?' he said in a hoarse whisper.

'That's right,' said Jane.

The driver made frantic signals to her to keep her voice down, looking over his shoulder as he did so.

'Great. Hop in.' he whispered, pushing the door ajar.   John could see four bodies in the back sprawled asleep among a jumble of black boxes of various sizes. He could just make out the name 'The Ready Teddys' stencilled on the side of the largest box.

'May we ask what for?' he whispered.

'Presumably,' whispered the driver wearily, 'being students you presumably know how to get to the students' union.'

'Presumably.'

'So presumably you'll be able to show us how to get there.'

'Couldn't we just give you directions?'

'Nah.   We've tried that.   Keep ending up in Bath for some reason.   The lads have threatened something horrible if they wake up in the wrong place again.   We're four hours late as it is.'

John sighed.

'OK.' He looked across at Jane. 'Do you want to come, or shall I meet you somewhere later.'

'I might as well come.   This shouldn't take long.'

The driver was not merely lacking in any sense of direction but tried to make up for it by constant creative effort, leaving no cul-de-sac un-explored.   As a result what should have been a five-minute journey took over half an hour, by which time the four in the back were beginning to wake up.

One of them emerged from the gloom and circled the driver's neck with his hands.

'Right, Dave,' he said, in a pleasant yet menacing tone, 'I have been delegated to enquire as to our whereabouts. If perchance we are not at the students' union by now, then I have also been delegated to tie a knot in your neck.'

John recognised the voice instantly.

'Hullo,' he said.

The delegate turned and looked at him blankly.

'Yeah?'

'We've met before,' said John. 'About a year ago. You played at the Christmas Dance at my school.'

John saw that Rick did indeed recognise him and Jane too after a swift scrutiny.

'Sorry, mate. Must have been someone else.'

A voice from the back room said,

'Yeah. Must have bin. You woz touring with Billy Fury last Christmas. That's what you told us at the audition anyway. Ain't that right, lads.'

Two voices mumbled agreement.

'I'm quite sure it was you.' John turned to Jane.' You recognise him, don't you? The bass player.'

Jane was unsure at first.

'I think so. I'm just trying to remember the name of the band. I certainly don't remember anyone mentioning Billy Fury. Let's see. What was it? The something Valley something. ... '

As she spoke John saw that Rick was gesticulating at her, out of sight of the others, trying frantically to get her to stop. He looked desperate for her not to remember.

'The Thames Valley Stompers'. That was it.'

There was a burst of hysterical laughter from the rest of the group.

'Stompers'? You bin playing in a fucking jazz band, mate? After all that guff about your uncle in the States, and how he makes all Bill Haley's stage gear?'

Rick had gone completely white, but said nothing until the laughter had died down. Then he reached across behind Jane and touched John lightly on the shoulder. As he did so, he put his lips near to Jane's ear and said, still looking at John,

'Tell your bird she's got it the wrong way round. It's mouth shut, legs wide… '

There was a stifled titter from the troglodytes in the back, as Dave got out and began unloading some of the equipment.

John suddenly heard himself saying,

'My bird can do what she likes, actually.'

Rick and Jane stared at him, equally astonished.

John watched himself get out of the van and pull Jane by the hand to follow him. He then slammed the door. He was astounded to find that Jane snuggled up to him as if seeking his protection. This was too corny for words. Any minute now he would begin drumming a victory tattoo on his chest. Since everyone else seemed deadly serious it was probably wise for him to keep as straight a face as possible. Otherwise he had a feeling that 'The Ready Teddys' might start mocking him and beating him up simultaneously.

As he and Jane walked away John made a private bet with himself as to when the next part of the ritual would be enacted. Probably at about fifteen paces, he reckoned.

He was only about a foot out.

They were about to turn the corner of the building, when he heard Rick say, with no great conviction,

'Just don't push it, that's all.'

This was followed by shouts of,

'That's right, Acker, you tell him.'

At the sound of laughter that ensued, John tightened his grip on Jane's hand and they made a run for the bus that was just approaching 'their' stop.

OVEREXPOSURE

Bristol, Winter

'Perhaps I should have hit him,' John had thrust his hands deep in the pockets of his donkey jacket.

'Don't be silly,' said Jane. 'There were four of them.'

'Three really. I don't think the driver was up to much.'

They were sitting at the table of the communal kitchen at the top of a tall narrow house overlooking the docks.

As far as the Gestapo-like University Accommodations Office was concerned it was an all-girl flat but it was actually one of a well-disguised chain of safe houses where pre- and occasionally extra-marital sex occurred from time to time. One of the girls and her unofficial live-in boy friend had gone to London for the weekend, which meant that John could have the spare room for the night.

'You don't look as if you could fight your way out of a rice pudding.'

The speaker was a short pugnacious looking girl who was rinsing her coffee mug out at the sink. Her hair was cut to resemble a black helmet and framed a pair of very dark eyes, which were staring at John contemptuously.

'Anica hasn't been in England long. She walked here from Romania.'

'Oh, I see,' said John. 'How long did it take you?'

'Four months.' Anica placed the mug carefully on the dish rack.

'I hope it was worth it,' said John.

His comment was deemed unworthy of a reply, and Anica walked out of the kitchen.

'Have I upset her?' asked John.

'Oh, no. She's always like that,' Jane reassured him. 'Especially to men.'

'I see.' John took a swig of his coffee. 'So I'll be safe here, as far as she's concerned.'

Jane frowned. 'Safe?'

'From assaults on my virtue.' John smiled.

Jane laughed.

'I thought your virtue was dead and buried months ago. You told me.'

John felt an overpowering urge to change the subject.

'Does Anica always wear black leather gloves to do the washing up?'

'Stop changing the subject,' said Jane, laughing

'No, seriously, does she?'

'Yes. But don't ask me why. She did say something once about being from the pre-revolutionary Romanian aristocracy, but I don't see how that that explains anything.'

'No. Bit odd, though.'

'Yes, almost as odd as you,' said Jane eyeing him over the rim of her coffee mug.

Anica strode back into the room. Her gloves were now matched by a pair of spike-heeled boots. She dropped into John's lap as if into a favourite armchair and put her boots on the table for Jane to admire.

'What do you think?' she asked.

'Anica, you're squashing him,' said Jane.

Anica reached round and patted John on the cheek.

'Your lover is fine, Jane. Aren't you?'

John made face at Jane over the top of Anica's head.

'Yes, fine. Happens all the time.' He searched Jane's face for any sign of jealousy. Anica wasn't totally bad looking, after all.

Jane was examining Anica's boots.

'What are they? Plastic?'

'Plastic?' shouted Anica. 'For a Constantinescou? Patent leather, darlink.' Anica stood up and performed a snatch of folk dance round the table and back to her armchair, which had crossed its legs in anticipation, so that she landed rather awkwardly.

Knowing that Anica was bound to comment on this, John tried a pre-emptive strike.

'I'm afraid I've got a bad leg.'

Anica shrieked with laughter.

'That's what the boys used to say in Romania! It was so sweet. One minute strolling along with their girlfriend, then suddenly ... old men. Bending over double, stopping for breath on a bench. All because of a little swelling.'

Anica reached behind her to pinch John on the cheek, and her finger slipped on a rivulet of sweat. She examined her finger for a second then swivelled round to look at him full face.

'Jane,' she said solemnly. 'I think your lover is a virgin.'

At this all three burst out laughing, each one of them for a different reason.

As abruptly as she had come in Anica announced that she had an essay to finish and left the room again.

John and Jane stared at each other rather awkwardly.

'Is she always like that?' asked John.

'Far worse, usually,' said Jane, smiling. 'She'd have had your trousers off normally.'

'What do you think stopped her?'

'I think she thought you were spoken for.'

'By you, you mean.'

'Yes.'

'Maybe her English isn't too good.'

'Oh, I think it is. Good enough.'

Jane looked straight at him for a moment and smiled. Then she got up in a decisive manner and took both their mugs to rinse them under the tap.

'Shall we go and sit in my room for a while? It might be quieter,' she said. 'We could listen to records or something.'

'As long as it's not the Beatles.'

'No. Promise. Although I'm quite tempted to go and see them this evening. They're at the Colston Hall.'

'Yes, I saw. We'd never get tickets though. They must have sold out weeks ago.'

'I think I could get hold of a couple.'

John felt a jolt of excitement, which he did his best to hide.

'Oh, really.'

'But only if you wanted. I wouldn't like to force you. I know what a purist you are.'

'I don't mind making an exception from time to time. In a good cause.'

'That's terribly noble of you.'

As they talked they had moved into Jane's room. As he sat down on the bed John took in the fact that he had never been to Jane's London equivalent. He looked around to see if the Bristol version was much different from David's description. This was one of the games they had played in the endless motel rooms across the States: Furnish This Room. In their mind's eye they had described in minute detail the rooms they had known in England and, when it had worked, homesickness, to which neither of them ever once admitted, crept off into a corner and hid for a while.

Everything seemed in order, the Françoise Hardy poster, the CND banner, the argumentative huddle of paperbacks by Sartre, Genet, Camus and all the gang.

There was of course nothing similar about the physical events taking place. David had described a series of endless skirmishes on this very bed cover, each one more torrid than the last. Except that the last never happened.

Did that mean he was about to be the first? Or did her changed outward appearance mean something?

Jane put on the Beatles LP. 'Please Please Me.' That must mean something, surely. She sat down at the other end of the bed. That must mean something, surely. He felt his penis give a little nudge. That must mean something, surely. She unpinned her hair and shook it down. That must mean something, surely. He tapped his feet to the music but huddled further into his bloody jacket. That must mean something, surely. She looked out of the window for a long moment, and then lit a cigarette. That must mean something surely. Neither of them spoke.

The door burst open and yet again Anica came in and strode over to the record player. She turned up the volume.

'Oh, I hoped I would be interrupting something by now. Don't stop on my account. There isn't much time before the concert.' She looked at John. 'You will be coming, I assume?'

'You're the one with the spare tickets? Is that it?' asked John.

'Spare tickets? No, but Jane has a source of supply I think. An admirer.'

'Just someone with a stupid crush on me. He's bought half a dozen tickets and wants me to go with him.'

'So the other four are up for grabs. If you're a good girl.' John was finding it increasingly difficult to seem uninterested.

'There's a good chance. He's promised one for Anica in return for certain favours, so I think I could manage to squeeze another one out of him.'

'In return for a few more favours.'

Anica picked up the aggrieved note in John's voice almost before he did himself. She hurled herself onto the sofa next to him and wrestled his head down onto her bosom.

'See, Jane, how jealous you are making your virgin lover. Perhaps it's better we cancel the whole thing.'

John made a vain grab to regain control of the helm. He extricated himself from Anica's embrace and tried to smooth down his hair, which was standing up in several spikes. He then tried to stand up, but then thought better of it and remained seated between the two girls. The authority of his

97

position was somewhat undermined by the fact that the bed sagged in the middle, which placed him perceptibly lower than his companions.

After a lightning quick calculation of the pros and cons, he decided that if he was going to lose his temper it had better be with Anica. She seemed after all to be the fly in the ointment at the moment.

'Look, Anica, let's get this straight.' He found that he was shouting. 'I'm not jealous, because I have absolutely no reason to be. I'm not Jane's lover because I … because I'm just not. And I'm not a virgin, either… not technically, any way.'
He immediately regretted the last few words and expected a tirade of cross-examination, from Anica if not Jane. To his surprise Anica appeared cowed by his speech and, getting up from the bed, she tiptoed out of the room, pausing only to turn the Beatles down to a faintly buzzing whisper.

After a further pause Jane ventured to speak.

'Do I take it then that you have no objections if we go to the concert with Martin?'

'Not particularly.'

'Only, he said he'd be round about six. We were going to have a drink first.'

'Fine.'

'Is there anything the matter?'

'Not really. I just wish you'd told me about this earlier. I seem to be in the way.'

'You're not!' Jane leaned across and squeezed his arm. That must mean something, surely. 'Honestly. I'd much prefer you and Anica to come. It would make it all less awkward.'

'Having two gooseberries, you mean.'

'Oh, for crying out loud.' Jane now stood up and put the faintly buzzing Beatles out of their misery and back in their record sleeve.

There was a ring on the doorbell followed by a sound like a large dog bounding up the stairs. Into the room burst, not Anica this time, but a fresh-faced bespectacled youth in a black corduroy jacket and trousers winkle picker shoes and a pink tab collar shirt. Before he registered John's presence he said, or rather sang just the 'OOOOH' from 'She Loves You' , complete with the head shake. Half way through this he noticed John, stopped and said,

'Oh, hello,' then swept his hair back into place and hitched up his trousers.

'Martin, this is John. The friend from home I was telling you about.' To John she sounded embarrassed. That must mean something, surely.

Martin came across to shake John's hand.

'Hello,' said John. 'Jane said you'd got a couple of spares for tonight.'

'Did she indeed, the naughty girl? I'm afraid they've gone. Awfully sorry.' He sounded genuinely upset at having to disappoint a friend of Jane's, of whichever sex. This must mean something, surely. John crossed Martin off his list of threats. Threats to what exactly, he wasn't yet sure. Threats to developing possibilities with Jane, perhaps. It would be a shame to disappoint Anica. Perhaps she'd like to come to see the Ready Teddys with him instead.

MR FAB

Bristol, Winter

Which was how, towards the end of their set, John found himself flat on his back in a clearing among the dancers, having ill advisedly tried to engage in some playful arm-wrestling with Anica.

After he had managed to stagger to the chairs at the side, and Anica had joined him after completing dancing to the number on her own, John said,

'Has she been going out with him for long?'

'Who? Martin?' Anica laughed. 'Never before.   This is the first time.' She took hold of John by the ears and turned his face towards her to examine his expression, as if studying the decoration on a vase. 'I think you are,' she said teasingly. 'Just a little bit. Jealous?'

***

In the Colston Hall the Beatles were coming to the end of their set.   There had been screaming from the moment that they stepped on stage and it had not been possible to hear more than a snatch or two of each song.   Jane was surprised how many she could recognise nonetheless.   Quite a few from the LP Martin had lent her plus songs she must have absorbed from the students' union jukebox.

Next to her Martin was beside himself. He could 'Twist'n'Shout' with the best of them, while remaining, like the vast majority of the audience, obediently in his seat. Jane smiled to herself.

Suddenly two very young girls sitting next to them at the end of the row, who had been screaming 'George!' and 'Paul!' all evening between collapsing into each other's arms in fits of weeping and giggles, made a break.   They ran down the aisle, swerving past the old commissionaire, and each threw something at their favourite Beatle. Jane could just make out a shower of what looked like multicoloured sweets, which Paul and George dodged with practiced ease. The two girls then ran back, again avoiding the commissionaire, and regained their seats.   The old man came up and tried to remonstrate with them but they paid him no attention so he wandered off again. This sortie seemed to have given the girls fresh energy, which they released by alternately jigging up and down in their seats and crying on each other's shoulders.

Jane wanted to attract Martin's attention to their behaviour, share her amusement with him.   But this was obviously no laughing matter for him.   His eyes were tight shut and he was pouring sweat.   But for the music one might have thought that he was having some kind of fit.   Perhaps he was.   Jane looked more closely at him.   He was smiling, which made it unlikely that he was actually ill.

About half an hour later, after the last scream had died, they were walking up the hill to the university.   Martin was holding her hand in his.   She felt it was the least, and preferably most, she could allow by way of thanks for the 'treat' as she called it, hoping that the word would compensate for the lack of gratitude in her voice.

'I'm so glad you enjoyed it,' said Martin.   He squeezed her hand tighter.   Jane tried to make it feel like a dead fish.   She really didn't want to encourage him.   She wondered what John was up to with Anica.

'Yes.   I don't think I've ever seen or heard anything like it. 'I'm still deaf from all that noise.' She looked across at Martin. 'You look absolutely worn out.   I thought you were going to have some kind of seizure in there.'

'I know. It really gets to me that music. I just can't help myself. I'll be all right soon. I thought John was fantastic, didn't you.'

Yes, amazing,' said Jane doubtfully.

'Don't tell me you can't tell them apart yet,' said Martin in mock chiding tones. 'He's the one with the sort of straight nose and half-closed eyes. Sings lead on 'Twist and Shout'.' Martin stopped in the middle of the pavement and adopted the John Lennon stance of legs slightly apart, leaning backwards a fraction, face up into the microphone.

'Well, come on, baby,
let's twist and shout.'

'Yes I remember now. I liked him.' Jane took the opportunity of Martin's performance to thrust both hands firmly in her coat pockets. A gaggle of Beatle fans who were passing managed to squeeze a last falsetto squeal out for Martin's benefit. On of them threw a small coin at his feet. He bowed, picked up the coin and resumed walking up the hill, his hands thrust deep in his own pockets.

'Does John mind my taking you out this evening?'

'Why should he mind?'

'I got the impression he might be an old boy friend.'

'No, he's just a friend of a friend. He went to school with my ex-boyfriend.'

'The one who's in America?'

'Yes. David.'

***

At about the same time the Ready Teddys were coming to the end of their set. There had been no screams or dodging multi coloured cascades of jelly babies. The moderate crowd had proffered friendly if not particularly enthusiastic applause at the end of each number.

Anica and John were in the balcony overlooking the dance floor.

'So you really go for this decadent Western music, do you?'

'Of course. Why not?' said Anica, who was looking over the edge of the balcony at the group. 'I like the guitarist. He looks like a very bad boy.'

'He tries to be.'

'You know him?'

'I've met him a couple of times.'

'Then you must introduce me to him.'

'I don't know him that well.'

'You mean you are just good friends?'

'Not exactly. He was the guy I nearly had the fight with this afternoon. The one I was talking about when you made your flattering remark about rice pudding.'

'Oh, yes I remember.' Anica laughed. 'Did I upset you?'

'Upset me? How could you possibly? I love being called a coward.'

Anica pondered for a moment, and then said,

'I think I am going to say hello.'

At this she got up and walked off along the row of seats to the Exit sign. John watched her disappear, and then a short time later, saw her approach the front of the stage and beckon to Rick. After a couple of double takes at the drummer he walked to the edge of the stage, still playing, and bent down to try to hear what she was saying. As she spoke he looked up to where John was sitting, then with a curt nod he got up and still playing resumed his proper place on stage, ignoring the singer's angry stare.

Five minute's later, just as John was deciding to go and look for her in the group's van, Anica returned.

'What were you saying to him?' asked John.

'Just inviting him to our party,' Anica said carelessly.

'What party?'

'I think we shall have a surprise party in our flat. For all the musicians in town.'

'All?'

'Yes, the Beatles too. Why not?'

John laughed.

'Have you asked them?'

'Not yet. You can phone them if you like.'

John decided that it was best to try and humour her.

'Sure. Why not? You've got the number of their hotel of course. If they're still in town, that is.'

Anica took a folded piece of paper from her handbag.

'Here. You must call this number and ask to speak to Mr Fab. It is not his real name.'

John rolled his eyes in disbelief.

'You don't say. Where on earth did you get all this from?'

'You don't believe me? Or are you scared again?'

John decided that perhaps a telephone call, even to someone called Mr Fab, was a small price to pay to reduce the surprisingly heavy burden of Anica's amused contempt. The fact that his arm still ached from their dance floor encounter earlier was an added factor.

'OK,' he said wearily. 'I'll do it, provided you come and hold my hand.'

Five minutes later Anica was all over him.

'You see, I told you. Now do you believe me?'

John shook his head in bewilderment.

'He certainly had the right accent and he did sound exactly like John Lennon. We'll just have to wait and see if they turn up.'

'You told him to bring a bottle?'

'Yes. I ventured to suggest the eight and sixpenny Yugoslav Reisling. I didn't know any Romanian wines.' Anica reached up and patted him on the cheek, saying nothing.

A few moments later a battered transit van drew up beside them and a head poked out.

'We're looking for the Hexagon.   Oh, hi, it's you again. We've been all over town looking for your party, but thanks to our driver here we keep ending up half way across the suspension bridge.'

For the second time that day John found himself clambering aboard the Ready Teddys' van. There was a kind of dream like inevitability to the operation, which anaesthetised him to any fear of the consequences. Rick seemed to feel the same, and said nothing for a moment, as if considering the position. Then he leaned towards Anica.

'You do know this geezer's been two timing you, don't you.'

Anica affected incomprehension.

'I'm sorry. I don't understand. Two timing?'

'Going out with other birds.   We caught him on the heath this afternoon with another tasty one. Dirty devil. Ran away before we could sort him out. Would you like us to do him over now? I know how you must feel.'

Anica screamed with laughter.

'Poor John. You're not even one timing, are you?'

Rick looked disbelieving.

'Don't tell me you're still just good friends. What's the matter with you? Don't like girls.   Is that it?'

Anica came swiftly to John's aid, although not quite as he would have wished.

'He loves them.   Perhaps too much, maybe.'

Rick frowned.

'Sorry.   I'm not with you.'

Anica smiled at him.

'Never mind.   That will never be your problem, I think.'

The van drew to a halt, and the driver said in disbelieving tones,

'Looks like we may be there.'

Anica looked out of the window.

'Yes, you are right.   But where are the Beatles?   They should be here by now.'

There was absolute silence for a moment, as if the Ready Teddys had suddenly realised they were out of their depth and were each wishing they were somewhere else.

Rick was the first to recover.

'Friends of yours are they?'

Anica said airily,

'Oh, no.   But as they're in town I thought it would be nice to invite them.'

John led the way up to the top of the house and into the kitchen, which was deserted. From Jane's room he could hear the sounds of the second Dylan LP. The door opened and Jane came out carrying a half empty bottle of wine. She was followed by Martin.

John swiftly scanned Martin's crotch for any tell tale lump and was relieved to find no evidence of any.

'Hello, how was the concert,' he asked.

'Very nice,' said Jane unenthusiastically.

'Oh, good,' said John, secretly relieved by her tone.

'They were absolutely fantastic,' said Martin. 'Especially Lennon,' he added.

'Not you and all,' jeered Rick. 'It's like a Poufs Palace in here. Don't tell me you're all Just Good Friends. I dunno how you girls manage.'

For the third time that day John felt like punching Rick in the mouth. This time he didn't restrain himself.

He was surprised in many different ways by his action: surprised how easily Rick fell over, surprised by the fact that the rest of the group didn't immediately beat him up, and, not least, surprised by Martin's reaction. While Anica and Jane rushed around with tissues and towels he blew John an exaggerated kiss.

SURPRISE ATTACK

Bristol, Winter

The three undamaged Teddys watched in stony silence as Rick sat up, dabbing his upper lip, and looked round at them.

'Thanks for your help, chums. Eternally grateful and all that.'

'We thought you could handle it.' The drummer said. 'I mean, a student … ' His voice trailed off into a quagmire of disdain.

'We could still jump him,' said the rhythm guitarist, taking a step forward.

'A surprise attack, you mean?' asked Rick sarcastically. He grinned at John, who couldn't help smiling back. 'We'd better lull him into a false sense of security first. Let's get this party on the road and then see. It'd help to get him pissed first.' Rick looked at John. 'What do you reckon?'

'Perhaps if I just apologised… ' John suddenly felt shaky, appalled at his own actions.

'Apologise?' Rick sounded aghast. 'And spoil all the fun?'

He came over and put his arm round John's shoulder, giving him a friendly squeeze. He looked round the room at no one in particular, then, raising his free arm in the air, pointed down at the top of John's head with one finger. 'Give this man a drink.' He pointed at himself, then each Teddy in turn,' And this man, and this man and this man.'

'There's food and drink in the kitchen,' said Anica. 'Why don't we all go in there?'

As they all filed out, the doorbell rang and a handful of guests trailed in. This process repeated itself at intervals over the next hour until there were perhaps thirty people circulating between the four rooms of the flat. They were mainly students with a sprinkling of younger members of the academic staff.

The Teddys had formed a circle near the drinks table from which one of them would thrust an empty glass towards any fellow guest who happened to be passing with a bottle in the hand. The percentage of those who were sufficiently intimidated to fill up the glass was pleasingly large.

John was just fetching a drink for Jane and was trying to edge past them back to the room where he had been dancing with her when a hand reached out and grabbed his glass. Was this the much heralded surprise attack, he wondered.

In an effort to defuse the situation he had been telling everybody in amused tones that the band were trying to get him drunk before attacking him and had tried to make a running joke of it with the group themselves. They had until now been quite amused, or so he had thought.

Rick was now looking at him completely impassively as he held out the glass.

'We think it's time you drank this. It'll help ease the pain.'

John clapped his hands for silence. One or two people stopped talking and looked round.

'Ladies and gentlemen, I am about to be beaten up. If any of you would care to intervene on my behalf I would be most grateful.'

Rick shook his head.

'No, no. We gave that the elbow. We've decided to play Cupid instead. Give this poor young lad one last chance to get his end away.'

'That's very nice of you, but I think I can manage in my own time, thanks.'

At this moment Jane, wondering what had happened to her drink, came into the room.

Rick turned to her.

'He says he can manage in his own time. Can you believe that.'

Jane wasn't clear what was going on.

'I'm sorry.   Manage what?'

'You.   Manage you, darlin' .'

John tried to indicate by the least eager expression he could muster, that this was not his idea and he was not interested in pursuing it.   He turned to leave the room but found his way barred by the drummer who was surprisingly nimble on his feet considering that he was by now a thin skin holding numberless pints that John could almost hear sloshing around inside him after he stopped moving.

'Course, if you don't fancy her, it's back to plan A.'

'Then it looks like it'll have to be plan A.'

Rick turned to Jane again.

'Quite a Galahad this one.   Says he'd rather get beaten up than, how shall we put it...'

'Shag me?'

'Any time, darlin'.'   There was a rumble of amusement from the Teddys.

Jane said nothing, but walked up to John, took him by the hand and led him out of the kitchen and into her bedroom, and after clearing the coats pushed John down onto the bed.

'Assuming they won't wait nine months,' she said,' what proof do you think they'll want? Perhaps we should enquire.'

' I think we should draw the line at eyewitnesses.   I don't think I could function in those conditions.   Assuming of course you want to go through with it.' Jane's reply suddenly seemed very important.

Jane considered for a moment.

'I think for the sake of appearances it would be best for you to emerge in about five minutes with a bloodied sheet. That seems to go down quite well in other parts of the world.   As for actually going through with it. ...' She paused again for thought.

Before John could answer there was a loud banging on the door.

'Orright, mate?' It was the drummer. 'Need any help?' This was followed by the sound of male laughter, interrupted by Anica's voice.

'Rick. Come away. Come away all of you. This is not funny any more. I am going to call the police.'

There was a staccato rap of smaller knuckles on the woodwork.

'John. Jane. Are you all right in there?'

John went to the door and said,

'Fine, thanks. We're just working out what to do.'

Anica sounded amused, despite herself.

'You know surely? In theory at least.'

Jane had come to the door.

'Of course we do, you idiot. It's just the proof we're worried about.'

'Ah, I see.' Anica pondered for a moment. 'I think I remember in one of my anthropology lectures there was a story about the whole community of a peasant village standing round the marriage bed to bear witness.'

'John doesn't reckon much to that. We thought a bloodied sheet would be easier,' said Jane.

'But that's only for virgins,' said Anica. 'I thought you told me … '

'I told you nothing, Anica,' said Jane severely, shooting an anxious glance at John.

'OK. Have it your way. I'll go and tell the others what to expect. How long will you be?'

'About ten minutes,' said John.

'My God! So romantic!' Anica exclaimed. They both listened to the sound of her boot heels fading away. John turned towards the bed and pulled the blankets back.

'Had you thought were we'd actually get the blood from?' asked John lightly.

'No, not exactly. I thought at first we could improvise something, with lipstick perhaps. But on reflection all I've got is Orange Blossom Special Gloss, which looks and smells exactly as you would expect.'

'Oh, well, it'll just have to be a jab in the finger with a needle. I don't mind.'

'Very noble of you, but there won't be enough blood to make it look convincing.'

'So what do you suggest, apart from the obvious.'

They were standing either side of the bed. Jane reached across and took John's hand, then sat down on the bed, pulling him with her.

'Let's try the obvious,' she said, and raising his hand to her lips began to gnaw gently on the knuckle of his forefinger.

To his astonishment John felt nothing in return. Even after lying down beside Jane and kissing her, stroking her breasts even, he felt detached and ill at ease. He wasn't sure how long he could go on pretending.

After a while Jane noticed something.

'Is anything the matter,' she asked.

'No, not really. I'm just feeling a bit pressurised. All those people out there. David … '

'David?' Jane drew away from him. 'What's he got to do with this?'

'Nothing, really. It's just that I said I'd keep an eye on you for him. See that you were all right.'

'And am I?' asked Jane. 'All right?'

'As far as I can tell.'

'Well then.'

John paused.

'I just feel I'd be betraying him, if we slept together.'

'And what about my feelings in all this? Don't they count for anything.'

'Of course they do.'

'Fine, good,' said Jane angrily. 'Well, you may be surprised to learn that tonight I feel like a good shag, OK? With you preferably, but … '

'Anybody, if necessary?'

'Sure.'

'So, I'm just a body to you?'

'More or less.'

John sat in silence for a minute.

'I'm sorry. I didn't realise how you felt. It's ironic really. Here you are, 'asking for it' as the saying goes, and here's me acting the shrinking violet. Only it's not acting.'

Jane sighed.

'So what happened to you with that girl in America? Put you off women or something?'

'No, not at all.' John felt himself blushing, and was glad the room was dark.

'So what's the difference? A rose is a rose is a rose, after all.'

'The difference is that no feelings were involved. I was just doing her a favour.'

'Very big of you, I must say.'

'No, really. She asked me to help her out and then things got a bit complicated.'

***

In the kitchen the Teddys were all lying with their heads under the drinks table like so many car-mechanics. Anica bent down to speak to Rick.

'Bloodied sheet? What are you on about?'

'They thought you might want proof.'

'Proof? That was just a wind up all that.' Rick rolled his head to speak to the others. 'Hear that, lads. old Peter Pan and Wendy? They thought we were serious.'

Anica stood up, poured herself another large glass, walked back to Jane's bedroom and knocked on the door.

'Hello. Jane, John. You can come out now, if you want. Rick was only joking.'

There was silence. After trying the handle, Anica waited for a moment, then shrugged and walked into the room where the record player was. Several couples were still dancing.

***

When Anica knocked, John had reached the same place where he had found Judy's cap. It had seemed the only thing to do. Better than laborious explanations. Jane was very quiet, not moving but trembling slightly as if there was something big spinning inside her.

As they heard Anica walk away, Jane whispered,

'I think you must have found something.'

Then she reached across and started unbuckling his belt.

As she did so John could feel that he was ready, although trapped at an awkward angle by the fabric of his jeans.

Another moment, and her hand was on him. Then she placed him where his hand had been before, and, still trembling, he began to move until he could not stop himself, but had to break cover and run for home, hoping with no certainty to find her waiting there.

FIST OF COINS

She must have been about twenty. Came bursting in to the pub to join her lunchtime drinking friends from some big city firm. Slapped a fist of grubby coins, mainly copper, on the table in the middle of all the glasses, and sat down quickly, beginning to count as she did so. No, she didn't want a drink.

Then he recognised her from yesterday. At the bottom of the steps beside the railway bridge. Smartly dressed and begging for money, with a real hunger for anything that was legal tender. No coin too small it seemed. He tried with a penny and she trembled as she thanked him. What was going on? She wasn't hungry, couldn't have spent very many nights in a cardboard box under Waterloo Bridge and come up looking like that. She didn't look addicted to any drug but money itself.

At the pub table she had almost finished counting and was being cheered on by her office colleagues.

'Ninety-eight, ninety-nine . . . ' they chorused. There was a moment's suspense as she rummaged in the cloth bag of the sort that banks use for small change. Nothing!

Then one of the crowd fished out a penny and held it tantalizingly before her. She tried to snatch it from him without success, until her tears of frustration shamed him and he allowed her to complete her pound.

1969

ANOTHER SWING OF THE DOOR

Jerusalem, Springr

Another swing of the door, another potted biography. Another life story, another swig of Stock. Another swig of Stock, another swing. Swig and swing. Cause and effect. How many more before this tiny town ran out?

Jane looked round the Puss-Puss club and wondered at the numbers of people there whom by London standards she knew intimately but had yet to meet.

Another swing. Silence. No word from Amnon.

Jane looked across at him. 'And?'

Amnon's brow wrinkled a fraction then his voice changed down almost imperceptibly to that sincere tone he used to use for especially elaborate lies. Although she was not the target this time, Jane's stomach flinched.

'Now this one is the Mystery Girl.' All Jane's new intimates had names in caps like characters in some modern Everyman. 'The Goat,' 'Naomi with the Glasses'.' She's a sabra, born on the Galilee kibbutz, works as a graphic designer and … '

Jane stared at the newcomer through the smoky air to make absolutely sure it was her.

'Is that what she's been telling you?'

Amnon grimaced and ducked his head slightly, holding his free hand above the table and rocking it left and right.

'Something she tells, some things I find out.'

'Not all pillow talk then?'

Amnon stifled a flattered smile. Another wrinkle on the forehead, another change of gear.

'Janey, do you want me to lie to you again. She was just a pig in a poke.'

'I'm sure she would be very flattered to hear you say that. Shall we ask her to sit with us?'

The wrinkles vanished for a split second as Amnon appeared to choke on his brandy. After some barely perceptible fumbling with the curtain a light conversational tone emerged.

'Sure. I'll go and ask her over.' Amnon got up and moved slowly over to the bar where 'Mystery Girl' was standing.

Jane watched the mime show of introduction, smiling to herself at the initial rejection, the renewed persuasion involving gestures towards their table, the weary glance, the double take, a look of shocked recognition, a nod of the head and a look of baffled triumph from Amnon.

'Hello. I thought it was you.' Jane, seated, felt in control as she looked up at Margaret as she reached the table. Amnon was still making his way through the crowd.

'Who's your friend?' Margaret motioned over her shoulder.

'It's rather a long story.'

Amnon had reached them and was awkwardly clutching three more large brandies and a jug of water. He gestured to Margaret to sit down,' Please.'

Jane moved along the bench to make room for her.

'Thank you.'

Amnon sat down opposite them, then distributed the glasses slowly, as if playing for time. A small squall of furrows chased across his brow.

Jane stole a glance at Margaret. Her mouth was straight across with just the tip of tongue showing. Maybe this was Sisterhood-at-play Time. Just a little revenge seemed too good a treat to miss. She leaned towards Margaret with a teeth clenched grimace, her hand extended.

'Hello, you must be the Mystery Girl Amnon's always talking about. Born on a kibbutz, graphic designer. All that. I feel I've known you for ages.' Amnon gave Jane a hard look, wiping his upper lip with the tip of his forefinger. Margaret took and held her hand for a moment.

'Delighted, I'm sure.' Margaret turned to Amnon.' Which kibbutz was it exactly? One is so forgetful about these things.' Trapped, Amnon took a long gulp on his glass studying both girls closely as he did so.

'Amnon remembers perfectly. Don't you, Amnon?' Amnon raised his hands in mock surrender, with a rueful smile.

'Galilee?' he asked.

'Galilee? No kidding. And here was I thinking I was just a poor black kid from Macon Georgia scrapin' a living with CBS television. Time I put away these fancy clothes and scrubbed out the cowshed.' She leaned closer to Amnon. 'Are we married, by any chance?'

'Oh no,' said Jane. 'Amnon assures me you were just a pig in the poke.'

'Just a pig in the poke.' Margaret might have been savouring a particularly complex vintage wine. 'Why, thank you, sir. With compliments like that I'll never feel insulted again. You mean sow, surely.' As she spoke, Margaret's smile grew wider and colder and her eyebrows slid slowly for cover under the leading edge of her afro.

'You must forgive me,' Amnon said, 'for using you to keep Jane amused. I would like very much to hear the truth from you.'

'So would I,' said Jane. 'Very much.' Margaret's eyebrows came out of hiding and lowered until she squint-frowned for a second. Then she said, 'If you go get us three more of those Golda Meirs, I'll tell you so much you'll be begging me to stop.'

'It's a deal.' Amnon made off towards the bar once more, crashing through couples as they danced hesitantly to 'Strange Brew' from -more raised eyebrows- the Cream's 'Disraeli Gears' album. The usual sound of accordion led folk songs had been interrupted after much insistence by a large young Englishman who had been shouting for 'Real Music' all evening, alternately clutching and brandishing the album in question like a cross between a piece of wreckage and a clove of garlic. This Englishman was now showing his affectionate gratitude by occasionally picking on couples as they danced and squeezing them together in an enormous and prolonged embrace.

Nodding towards 'Bearhug' as Jane had already nicknamed him, Margaret asked, ' Is he with you?'

'Do me a favour!'

'And drop dead? Is that what you mean?'

'I wouldn't put it quite as strongly as that.'

' Look, if it's about that time with David … '

'That time with David? You make it sound like a day out. Just another pig in the poke, as Amnon would say. You came damn close to wrecking my life 'that time with David.' We were perfectly happy till you came along.'

Margaret sighed softly. 'That ain't the way he told it, honey.'

Jane was still angry. Trying, suddenly, not to cry with rage. 'And of course you had to believe his word against mine. Except that you never heard my side of the story.'

'Did you ever hear mine?'

'No, but David spoke about you endlessly at the time.'

Margaret paused for thought, gave a little decisive nod of the head and leant towards Jane to make herself heard against the steadily increasing volume of the music. 'Bearhug' had obviously squeezed the regular DJ into a coma if not temporary death and now had the run of the turntables.

'OK … now … here comes Mizz Roosevelt's New Deal. Let's both of us cut out the middleman an' tell it like it was for us. What do you say?'

Before Jane could answer Amnon returned with the drinks.

'Here we are, girls. Three treble Goldas.'

He placed the three tall glasses on the table and, supported himself on two of them like little crutches as he pivoted round and down onto his seat.

Jane took a glass and thought for a moment.

'What do I say? I say, here's mud in your sty.'

As she spoke she raised her glass to Amnon, who cocked his head at both girls, like a dog about to 'fetch.'

SUPERSOL BOMB

Jerusalem, Spring

Shortly after her first visit to the Puss-Puss club, Margaret was browsing through the shelves of the Supersol supermarket, looking for something for supper. Her wire basket was half full as she hesitated over an elderly looking tin of stuffed peppers.

Suddenly she heard the wail of sirens and the screech of brakes directly outside. Men were running from cars towards the shop, shouting urgently in Hebrew to the handful of customers inside, who looked bemused at first but then started making their way rapidly to the checkouts. Still not understanding, Margaret followed.

Seeing her puzzled expression a policeman beckoned to her from the shop door way.

'You must come. There is bomb. Stand by the car. Hurry.'

Margaret added her basket to the heap by the checkouts and, trying not to panic, moved as quickly as she could towards the cars. Her instincts told her, screamed at her, to move much farther away, but she found that she was penned in, perhaps deliberately, with the other shoppers by a triangle of cars. As she searched in vain for a means of escape, she saw Amnon. He was standing a little apart, looking intently at his watch.

'Hey, Amnon!'

He looked up briefly, registered her presence and then looked back at his watch.

Margaret pushed her way towards him through the pen.

'What's happening? It's me, Margaret. Don't you recognise me?'

Without taking his eyes from his watch, Amnon raised his hand in a gesture designed both to acknowledge and to silence her.

Suddenly from within the shop there was a bright yellow flash, and a muffled explosion followed by what sounded to Margaret like a chandelier in some distress. Then there was silence for a moment as a pall of black smoke began to drift slowly through the shattered plate glass frontage. Margaret turned back in time to see Amnon give a nod of the head and a fleeting smile of satisfaction.

In that moment he became once more the affable night clubber of recent memory and strolled over towards her.

'Hello, again.'

'Oh, you're talking to me again, are you? Do you mind telling me what the hell is going on.'

'There has been an explosion.'

Despite the fact that her knees had begun to tremble, Margaret tried very hard to match his lightly bantering tone.

'No kidding! Any idea who the dissatisfied customer could be? The PLO?'

'It could be. We don't know yet.'

While they were speaking, police had begun to cordon off the area and to question those shoppers capable of speech. Others, still in shock, were trying to retrieve their baskets and having to be restrained. They protested vigorously to the officer in charge, who shrugged wearily and beckoned to the storeowner. He in turn, though still very dazed, came over to one of the checkouts and began ringing up the goods. A queue formed, with a certain amount of ill-tempered jostling. The small crowd of onlookers behind the police barriers gave a small, half ironic, round of applause.

Amnon, who had been watching these developments with his usual air of a connoisseur of human foibles, turned to Margaret and said, 'And how about you? Don't you want to get your groceries too?'

'I seem to have lost my appetite all of a sudden.'

'Oh, I'm so sorry.'

As the shoppers came away from the checkout, they were being escorted, still clutching their baskets, to a large bus which had drawn up outside. One of the policemen manning the cordon came over to Margaret and said something abrupt to her in Hebrew, at the same time taking her by the elbow as if to drag her towards the bus. As he did so, Amnon said something that sounded to Margaret like 'OK,' and pulled about a quarter of an inch of blue plastic card from his outside breast pocket. The policeman raised his eyebrows and gave a nod of understanding, before letting go of Margaret's elbow and returning to shepherding potential witnesses onto the bus.

'That was very impressive,' Margaret said.' What was it? Your Diner's Club Card?'

'Not quite.'

'Whatever it was, it was certainly a neat trick. Looks like it's saved me a whole lot of trouble with those guys, what with me not understanding the questions and them not understanding the answers. What was the magic password, by the way?' Amnon looked puzzled. 'The one you used before you pulled the plastic on him. Sounded exactly like 'OK' to me.'

'It was.' They both laughed and then Margaret said,

'It was probably the way you said it. While you're at it, any chance of getting me out of here?'

'Sure.' Amnon began to pull the end of the barrier to make a gap for her. There was a flurry of interest from one or two of the policemen by the bus, but the one who had approached Margaret reassured them that everything was 'OK.'

As she walked free Margaret felt her knees buckle. She grabbed Amnon's arm.

'I think I need to sit down for a while.'

'Sure. Maybe you would like to lie down. My flat is quite close by.'

'Thanks, but I'll take a rain check on that, if you don't mind.'

'I have another suggestion. Would you like a drink?'

Margaret laughed weakly,
'One of your triple-decker Goldas? I don't feel quite ready for that. I could manage a lemon tea, though.'

***

About twenty minutes later they were both squeezed around a formica topped table in Ta'amon, a small perpetually crowded coffee bar favoured by artists and writers.

There was a particularly vociferous exchange of views taking place between two of the tables and the man working the coffee machine. Amnon was obviously dying to get involved, but out of consideration for Margaret held back, apart from one or two brief interjections. With her spoon, Margaret squeezed the last drop of flavour from her tea bag against the side of the glass and pulled it out by its string and lowered it, spinning very slowly, onto the gutted slice of lemon in the saucer. Amnon was hunched over his second cappuccino, stirring the sprinkling of chocolate methodically into the froth.

'That's what I find so frustrating,' Margaret said.' Being in a country that's wall-to-wall talk and not being able to eavesdrop, let alone participate, because I can't understand a damn word.'

'Apart from 'OK'.' Amnon gave her a teasing look over the rim of his cup.

'I'm serious. It's like watching a shoal of fish all going along together, and then, for no reason, except the reason they all know about, switching course and heading in a completely new direction.' Margaret sipped the last of her tea. The dregs were suitably bitter. 'I mean,' she adopted the tones of a boy she remembered from school, 'I'm acustomised to bein' hip, you dig?'

'I can translate for you. No problem.'

'When your other duties permit, I take it?'

'Sure.'

Margaret felt certain that her next question would be pointless, but she had to try.

'And what are those other duties, exactly?'

Amnon was half way through draining his cup. He finished doing so and put it carefully back on the saucer, then centred it exactly.

'I tell you one day.'

'One day?'

The nightclub seducer returned, to comically exaggerated effect.

'The day the dawn discovers us together?'

Margaret giggled. 'Looks like a long wait … for both of us.'

Amnon cocked his head as if acknowledging an elegant move across some chequered board.

'We see … Something more to drink?'

'No, thanks. I must get back. I've got some work to do for a production meeting tomorrow.'

'Television?'

'Yes. It's a documentary on the way Israel was created, the events leading up to '48. Kind of a coming of age profile. I really need to talk to people who were around then to get all that history off the page and into the heart.'

Amnon looked wryly delighted. 'So they pick a black American girl without a word of Hebrew?'

'They picked me for my track record, not the colour of my skin.'

'And the Hebrew?'

'I'm sure you'll manage that.'

Temporarily outmanoeuvred, Amnon's smile broadened.

'You have a deal … On one condition.'

'Yes?'

'You come to my party tomorrow night.'

Gathering up her coat and tote bag from the back of her chair, Margaret stood up.

'OK, you smooth talking sabra … '

'Two words of Hebrew now. Many congratulations!'

' … you've talked me into it. The party, that is.'

'STRANGE BREW . . .

Jerusalem, Spring

'Strange brew, girl, what's inside of you?' Jane hummed softly to herself.

Amnon's party was this evening. Since his tiny flat wasn't big enough for the '48 and '67 generations to mingle comfortably, Jane had been persuaded to 'volunteer.'

It was for this reason that she was wandering about in the old three-roomed Arab house, a domed entrance hall/dinning room flanked by bedroom and drawing room, trying to decide where to put things.

Just as she was deciding to leave everything to Amnon when he eventually turned up, the doorbell rang.

'Come in. It's open.'

Nothing happened.

'It's open.'

There was the sound of a gentle moaning from outside.

Jane ran to the door and tore it open. At first she saw nothing, then looking down saw Bearhug lying curled up at her feet, his hands folded under his head in classic 'up wooden hill to blanket fair' style. His feet were resting on one corner of the swirling psychedelia of the Cream's 'Disraeli Gears' album. Bending down, Jane gently shook his shoulder. Although it was only late morning, Bearhug reeked of alcohol. Quite a night, obviously.

At the touch of her hand, and with his eyes half closed he rolled onto his front and half stood up. Just as he was about to fall flat on his face again, his legs took what appeared to be an independent decision to lead the way past Jane and into the house. In passing, and not to be outdone by mere legs, an arm shot out and placed the album with astonishing delicacy and accuracy in Jane's hands.

As this anarcho-syndicalist movement spread, Jane, who was riding the slipstream, managed to detect mumbled fragments of vocal product. Each seemed as devoid of meaning as single elements of morse.

'Pro muzichairsh . . . . Amno sed bee lay . . . . Thor cumelp . . .'

Jane was beginning to wonder how to prevent a head on collision with the dining room wall (a rugby tackle perhaps?) when, with the merest hint of a hand signal, The Assemblage took a left and made a running dive onto Jane's bed.

'Lih sleeh . . . beh sooh.'

A large hand thrashed briefly like an expiring haddock.

'Nye nye.'

'You can't stay here. I've got work to do.' Jane's words sounded half-hearted and unconvincing even as she spoke them. The Assemblage was quite unmoved.

Jane walked over to the record player, with the idea of blasting Bearhug awake with strong dose of his beloved Cream. She was pondering which track might best fit the bill when she heard a light tap on the front door and the flip-flop sound of sandal on stone.

Jane turned to see Margaret, looking considerably more 'down home' than she had the previous evening.

'Oh, hi … This where the party is?'

'That's right.'

Margaret had stopped in the middle of the central room and was doing a slow three hundred and sixty degree turn to take everything in. She paused a fraction when she saw Bearhug sprawled on the bed but made no comment.

'You're a bit early, I'm afraid,' said Jane.

'Oh, I know. I thought I'd come and help you guys out. Where's Amnon? He told me he'd be here.'

'According to his wing-ed messenger in there,' Jane gestured towards the bedroom,' he's going to be late.'

'Has he been living with you long?' asked Margaret, nodding towards The Assemblage.

'Him? Oh, no. He doesn't live here. He's only been here five minutes. I don't know where he lives.'

'Uh-huh.'

'It's quite true.'

'Oh, I believe you. Not really your style.'

Jane said nothing. There was an awkward silence as Margaret walked around looking closely at the house, pausing occasionally to examine a particular feature at greater length.

Eventually Jane said,' You reckon you're an expert on my style, do you?'

Margaret put down a cushion whose embroidery she had been admiring, and turned to face her.

'You still angry with me? After all these years?'

'Does it show? I'm sorry.'

'You wanna talk about it?'

'What good would that do?'

Margaret shrugged resignedly and continued her inventory of the house, concentrating this time on Jane's record collection.

Jane began sweeping the floor, and the sound of the brush merged with the sorting of records.

'You've got some mighty strange stuff here,' said Margaret, and she began reading out the label of a record she was holding, a 45 rpm single in a grubby white sleeve. Her voice rose in amused disbelief as she read.' Good-bye, England, Good-bye? . . . The Neverly Brothers? . . . Nutcase Records?' She laughed out loud. Jane swept harder, knocking the broom against the legs of the dining room table.

'This I've got to hear. Do you mind?'

Without pausing in her work, Jane said,

'No. Fine. Go ahead.'

Margaret put the record on. There was a brief crackle from the run in groove, and then.

130

'Awopbopaloobopalopbamboom!'
'Hello, everyone. That was John being spontaneous …'
As the record played Margaret turned slowly towards Jane, who continued sweeping but gradually more slowly and mechanically.

At first Margaret seemed unable to believe her ears and watched Jane's movements for some sign of confirmation.

'That's it, folks … Phew … Are we still … '

Jane, who had stopped sweeping, slowly looked up at Margaret, who said softly,

'Was it? … Them?'

Jane nodded slowly.

Margaret shook her head in disbelief.

'They sound so incredibly young. I can't believe it's only been six years.'

'I don't know why I've hung on to it,' said Jane as she bent to scoop up the small triangle of dust at her feet. With the edge of the dustpan, which had become knife sharp with use she sliced it from the floor. Her movement started quick and clean then slowed in the upward curving follow through.

'It seems to have clung on like some kind of unwelcome heirloom,' Jane went on. 'I'm surprised how upsetting it is to hear it, even after all this time.'

'Me too.'

'I find that hard to believe,' said Jane.

'How come?'

'You were the winner.'

'Hold on a minute, honey child. Who said anything about winning?'

'According to David's letter you were.'

'Oh, sure. Sounded like. But it sounds to me like the deafening roar of male self-justification. You and me never got a chance to speak.'

131

Jane was still holding the dustpan and began to cradle it as she crossed her arms loosely in front of her.

'But I didn't want to speak to you.'

'Yeah, I know, David kept telling me how angry you'd be.' Margaret rolled her eyes in mock terror. 'So I decided to lie real low. I'm sorry for that now. I felt I had no choice.'

Jane smiled bitterly.

'No, let me guess,' she said.' You were just obeying orders. You do realise that excuse doesn't work any more. Especially in this country.'

' No, I started in of my own free will. And I got what I wanted, mainly.'

'Bully for you,' said Jane.' So what's the problem?'

'The problem is that we should have had this conversation long ago. Maybe we would have if it wasn't for the BBC.'

Jane looked puzzled.' The BBC?'

Sure. How does it go now?' Margaret began to speak in measured tones. 'Nation shall speak unto nation.' Fine, no problem. But, woman unto woman? No way. Thanks to the BBC … Boys' Bullshit Conspiracy.'

' ... GIRL, WHAT'S INSIDE OF YOU?'

Jerusalem, Spring

Jane turned and emptied the dustpan into a pedal bin just inside the kitchen door. Then she came and sat down at the table.

'So now's your chance. I'm all ears.'

Margaret sat down at the table opposite her.

'That's just the problem. Too much listening. We've both done too much listening. I can't speak unless you tell your side. I need to know what you were thinking and doing then.'

Jane bowed her head briefly and then looked up at the ceiling.

'I don't think I could go through with that. It would be too painful ... Old wounds ... As far as I'm concerned, both John and David are dead.'

'And you with them?'

'Where do you Yanks get it from?' Jane said sharply. 'All these yards and yards of fire damaged Freud. Special off the peg discounts to fit every psyche. They must have a whole warehouse at UCLA somewhere. That was where you were actually studying, wasn't it?'

Margaret smiled at her.

'The Kraken wakes. I knew someone was home.'

'You ... fucking ... bitch!' said Jane slowly.

Margaret stood up and moved round the table to put an arm around Jane's shoulders. Jane said nothing, but pushed Margaret away with one arm.

As she did so, Margaret grabbed her by the wrists and pulled Jane round to face her.

'Jane, will you listen to me?'

Looking down at the floor away from Margaret, Jane stiffened. Then, in a calm singsong, she said,

'Let go, please. Let go of my wrists, you're hurting me.'

'Will you please listen to me?'

'Thought I wasn't allowed to listen. Might stop you rediscovering your past.'

'Let me just say one thing?'

'Talk till you're blue in the tits. I can't stop you. You've wrecked my life so far. Why not finish the job?'

'You flatter me, sister. I think you deserve just a little credit.'

Jane stood up, breaking free of Margaret's grip on her right wrist. With her free hand Margaret pulled Jane's chin round in an attempt to establish eye contact. Jane shook her off and took a couple of paces backwards and then stopped in a boxer's crouch.

Margaret folded her arms in front of her and settled her weight on her back foot. Jane moved towards her.

'Now, listen, you bitch,' she said. 'After this, I don't want to listen to you, I don't want to talk to you, and I don't want to see you. The only reason I *am* talking to you is to shut your fucking mouth, stop you from explaining everything, stop you from rationalising everything, stop you from blaming me - ME! - for what you did ... '

Margaret wiped a fleck of Jane's spittle from her own face.

'I'm sorry, you're spraying me.'

'You're sorry ... *you're* sorry? Hogging the blame a little, aren't we? Well, get your grovelling gob round *this* ... '

Jane spat full in Margaret's face. Margaret remained impassive as the spittle slid down her cheek and began to collect under her chin before dripping down the front of her dress. Jane looked stunned by her action and reached slowly out to touch Margaret's face. Margaret said nothing and Jane withdrew her hand half way.

Jane tried to speak,

'I ... I'm ... '

'Sorry?'

'I said ... '

'No, you didn't. And don't. Ever. There's a better way.'

'How do you mean?'

Without a word, Margaret handed her a white handkerchief that she had tucked in at her wrist. Jane took it and began, hesitantly at first, to wipe Margaret dry. When she had finished she handed back the handkerchief.

'Feeling better now?' asked Margaret.

'A little… And you?'

'I was fine to start with.'

'No, I mean … after … what I did?'

Margaret shrugged,

'I've had worse. You did it, then you undid it. Finito. Wiped clean, like any other black slate. Just don't apologise. This is strictly business.'

'If that's how you feel.'

Jane picked up the tablecloth from the floor and began covering the bare wood. As she did so, she went on,

'I just don't understand what you want from me. You deny any guilt, you won't let me apologise, and you won't forgive. What else can I do?'

The cloth was smooth, the corners trimmed.

Margaret leaned on one corner of the table with one arm supporting her, and rocked gently to and fro, using the arm as a pivot. After a while she said,

'You could try looking.'

'At what?'

'Me … You. Me and you.'

' What's the point of that?' Jane asked, and began to walk towards the record player.

Before Margaret could reply, The Assemblage slouched past between them, still trailing the debris of human utterance like rubbish tipped from the back of a cross channel ferry.

'Wezzabog? … Mussavvapee … ' Bearhug took a short turn at the helm. 'Where's the music? Should be dancing.' He had just managed to spread his arms and make a brief stumbling step towards Jane and Margaret when The Assemblage regained control. A perfect three-point turn was followed by an immaculate approach run and the slamming of the bathroom door.

Margaret smiled.

'I can't believe that guy. He must be on auto-pilot or something.'

'No. Just good old Stock Fine Cognac. At least a gallon I should say.'

Margaret was still smiling as she asked,

'Anyway, what makes you think you've hurt me?'

'Do you like being spat at?'

'No. But it's happened before.'

When you were a kid, I suppose.'

'No, my childhood days in Macon, Georgia were remarkably devoid of such salivary tributes. I'm talking about someone you knew. Someone with a positive adoration of the black race, someone who, despite not being blessed with the same pigmentation, idolised one particular brother, one particular vocalist … '

' John? I don't believe it!'

'You better, babe. 'cause it's true.'

Jane shook her head slowly.'I don't understand. Why would John want to do that?'

Margaret sighed,

'He never told you?'

'No. Nothing at all. What happened? You must have done something to upset him.'

'Yes, I must have done. I mean, I did.'

'What was it?'

Margaret leaned forward and scratched at a small stain on the cloth with her thumbnail. Jane watched as she failed to remove the stain. A damp cloth was what was needed. Jane had one somewhere.

Margaret sounded embarrassed as she answered Jane's question.

'I regret to say that I called him a faggot. Or rather I implied that he was.'

'You didn't!' said Jane. 'What on earth made you say that?'

'All the people he admired were black homosexuals.'

'So you called him a queer - sorry, faggot.'

'Yes,' said Margaret.' It makes me very embarrassed to think about it now. I had no evidence.'

'Either way?' said Jane with studied carelessness.

With a final brushing motion with the tips of her fingers Margaret turned her full attention to Jane.

'Either way.'

Suddenly there was the sound of a stylus making series of high volume crash landings on the surface of a record.

'She's a witch of trouble in electric blue,

in her own mad mind she's in love with you,

with you … '

They both stood up and turned to where the sound was coming from. Bearhug, in what looked like a rather longer period of remission than before had turned away from the record player and was staggering towards them. His arms were wide apart as he closed on them, squeezed them together with a huge wordless smile in a double turn, and then spun off at a tangent, with a little help from The Assemblage, back towards the record player.

Still pink from laughter, the two women continued to turn in a loose embrace. Their movements coincided with the music without it being possible to say that they were actually dancing to it. When it stopped they continued to revolve under their own momentum for a few seconds until coming to a halt.

Before they could disengage there was the sound of another crash landing, this time on the riff intro to 'Sunshine of Your Love.' This time they did not need Bearhug's physical assistance as Margaret took the lead.

'You knew what I was feeling, then,' Jane said.

'I had an idea.'

'And you?' For the first time, Jane looked deep into Margaret's eyes, and then with a slight smile she shook her head. 'No, I don't think so. Never mind. Plenty more fish in the sea.'

Margaret twirled Jane round and said teasingly,

'You dykes are all the same.'

'Is that what I am?' asked Jane. 'A dyke? Doesn't sound much fun. I'm not sure I want to play this game.'

Margaret twirled Jane again until she was in her embrace and then gave her a big hug.

'Don't worry, you'll be fine.'

At that moment Amnon arrived in the hall doorway. As Jack Bruce sang, he watched the two main women in his life dancing together, without his permission.

DUSK

*Sometimes on summer evenings I grew tired
of playing soldiers. The rows of men upon
the tabletop held little fascination
compared to the new established ritual of
the outside dusk.*

*The boy across the road would kick a
football against the wall of his house.
Over and over again. Then the wooden door
under my window would scrape and creak and
there would be a scrap of conversation.
'No, mummy, I won't be late.' Then light
steps down the path. I saw nothing. Heard
only the few more football plastic
bouncings, then silence.*

*Later when we stood around in our little
roller skating group, talking before
supper he tried to fight me to the ground.
Because she was there. Because he was a-
bristle at the thought of threat from me.
I don't know what I did. Maybe I should
ask him now. Could he tell me now?*

*So as the summer grew they withdrew
into themselves, broke up the group. I
didn't come out again very often. Just
bought more soldiers and increased my
command of military language from a bygone
age.*

*Mum and Dad seemed pleased somehow that
I wasn't up there with any body living.
Apart from rows of grenadiers reliving
history.*

*I did bring someone back home once. It
was a mistake actually. In every sense of
the word.*

We got talking over a box of hussars in one of the specialist shops and I invited her back to see my collection. I was looking at Waterloo, I think. Dear old Mum got completely the wrong end of the stick and gave the poor girl the full treatment. I was about nineteen at the time and she was getting a bit worried about the fact that I was giving her and Dad no worries. So . . . it was cups of tea every quarter hour, in depth interrogation about her background, were her intentions honourable (well you know what I mean). Finally I just lost my temper and burst into tears. The girl got really embarrassed and beat a hasty retreat. I never saw her again and Mum and Dad never mentioned it.

CIVILIAN CASUALTIES

Jerusalem, Spring

It was after midnight and Amnon's party was winding down. Several of the guests were sitting round the table discussing the Supersol bomb and who might have been behind it.

Apart from Jane, Amnon and Margaret, there were Max and Lotte from the '48 generation and Ilan and Naomi from the '67 generation. Ilan was recovering from a recent operation on a leg injury sustained in the Six Day War. Naomi, his girlfriend, was a graphic design student. Out of politeness to Jane and Margaret everybody was speaking English for the most part, except when the discussion got particularly heated.

Max narrowed his eyes against the smoke of his cigar.

'What is the logic?'

Ilan gestured impatiently.

'You want logic from terrorists? They just want to kill.'

Max raised an eyebrow and removed a fragment of cigar leaf from the tip of his tongue.

'Kill? With a smoke bomb in an empty supermarket?'

'Just bad planning,' Ilan said, in Hebrew. 'Like all these Arabs.'

Amnon leaned over and said to Jane and Margaret, in a stage whisper, 'Can you understand what they are saying?'

'All except the Hebrew,' said Jane, loud enough for Ilan to hear.

Ilan stopped, looked a little aggrieved, and then with a slightly surly tone, said,

'Oh, sorry. I will try to speak like your English queen.'

Naomi, leaned across and hit him on the head with a bendy yellow plastic hammer that made a high pitched squeak as the blow landed. Ilan swatted her away with an indulgent smile.

'You can speak like our President too, if you like,' Margaret said. 'Anyway, how come you call them terrorists? The Palestinians have every bit as much right to a homeland as the Jews. Nobody here would call the Jews terrorists for bombing out the British and driving out the Arabs when all this was Palestine. They're heroes now. All of them. Irgun, Stern Gang ...

Max reached out to stub out his cigar.

'Not all heroes,' he said quietly. 'Not quite.'

Lotte looked at him anxiously as if she saw trouble ahead.

'Max,' she said softly.

Naomi, who had been listening to the conversation while appearing to be testing her reflexes by banging the hammer on her knee, interrupted.

'But against the British was different. A colonial imperialist power deserved to be under attack. Sure some Arabs got a bad deal, but,' Naomi shrugged, ' it couldn't be helped.'

Jane felt she had to speak.

'So you're saying that two rights, the rights of the Palestinians and the rights of the Jews, led inevitably to a wrong. And the wrong against the Palestinians is just too bad?'

Naomi sighed. 'Listen ... Ilan was nearly killed fighting for our country. Our country. You want us to give it back?' She turned for support to Max. 'Max, you tell her. You fought for independence in '48. You weren't terrorists ... To the British, maybe.'

Max was still lost in his own train of thought. He said slowly, 'To the British? ... Of course. To ourselves? Not then ... But now?'

Margaret spoke eagerly but softly,

'Are there things you regret?'

Before he could answer, Lotte touched him on the arm and said,

'Max, darling, it's getting late. We should be going.'

142

'All right, Lottchen, in a minute.' Having surfaced from his reverie to answer her, he resumed his semi-soliloquy. 'Regrets? … The ends, no … The means, perhaps … A homeland for the Jews, of course … but civilian casualties … ' Max lapsed into thoughtful silence.

'Civilian casualties?' Ilan looked puzzled and slightly indignant. 'My father always said that you were under strict instructions to attack only military targets.'

'He told you that?' Max gave a wry smile.

'You mean there where deliberate attacks on civilians, British civilians?' Margaret said. 'Can you be specific?'

Max sighed. 'This is all old history.' He patted Lotte's hand, which was still resting on his arm and made as if to stand up. 'You can look it up in the Jerusalem Post. It's all there.'

'The bare facts, maybe,' said Margaret. 'But not the… logic? … behind the attacks.'

'Unlike yesterday's illogical attack, you mean?' added Jane.

Ilan rounded on her angrily,

'You are for terrorism? Is that what you are saying? Maybe you want I should lose this completely.' He pointed at his damaged leg.

Jane held her ground. 'No, of course not. But I need the truth. I need to know the difference … between now and then, between today and yesterday, between freedom and terror … '

'Between black and white, between chalk and cheese?' Max was smiling at her.

Jane flushed. 'I'm serious.'

Naomi said calmly, 'Why does it matter so much to you. You don't live here. You have nothing here.'

'That's right. I don't live … here. I have nothing … here.' She felt her eyes stinging with tears. 'This is where I feel these things most strongly. And yet I was born here, and my parents died for your country here.' Ilan was a blur as she turned towards him and smiled. 'Not a bad pedigree, wouldn't you say?'

In Ilan's voice awed respect battled with disbelief. 'Your mother and father were Jews? Freedom fighters?'

'No. As far as I can gather they were lapsed agnostics and very minor civil servants in the British administration. Issuing parking permits for camels, I expect. Very humdrum.'

Naomi didn't smile. 'But you said they died for our country?'

Jane took a deep breath.

'Yes, they did exactly that. But not in the heroic way you imagine. They were simply shot dead on the street on the way home from the cinema one evening, but, in so far as their demise preceded, by a year or so, the British withdrawal from Palestine and the establishment of the state of Israel, you could say that they did, quite literally, die for your country. Their deaths helped to breathe life into Israel.' Jane lined up a fork and a wine glass, shutting one eye as she did so. 'I think they would have liked it here, if anybody had bothered to ask them to stay. But nobody did.' She laughed softly to herself. 'Except of course that they did stay. They're buried here. Somewhere. Part of the scenery, you could say.'

'Do you know where?' Lotte asked.

Jane looked at her. 'Mount Scopus? That's what I've been told.'

'And have you been there?' Lotte asked again.

Jane picked up the fork and began to ping the tines, touching the other end on the tablecloth and releasing the resulting note into the wine glass with her other hand. It was a trick her foster father had taught her when she was very small.

'I've thought about it, but there doesn't seem any point, somehow. I can hardly remember them, so I don't see what good staring at a slab of stone is going to do. It's over and done with.'

'Or just begun, maybe,' Margaret murmured.

144

Jane stopped in mid ping.

'Sorry, I don't get you.'

'Oh, nothing.'

Max lit another cigar.

'May I ask, what were the names of your mother and father?'

'Daventry … James and Selina Daventry.'

'Ah, yes.'

Margaret darted in. 'You knew them?'

'I had dealings with them once.'

Jane looked surprised. 'Once? I'm surprised you remember after so long.'

Margaret was observing Max's expression very closely.

'Just a routine matter. I never knew their names … But when I read the story in the Post it shook me. It made me lose a little faith.'

'In routine?' asked Margaret quietly.

Max looked up at her.

'Routine. Yes,' he said slowly.

***

Two hours later Amnon was walking with Margaret past the floodlit walls of the Old City.

After a silence Margaret said,

'Tell me about Max.'

'Sure. If you will tell me about Jane.'

Margaret laughed. 'Always the deal, right? I was forgetting. What's the problem? You've known her long enough to make a few informal guesses based on your intelligence. You don't need my help. However, if you can help me with my programme, I'm willing to discuss terms.'

'My terms are very simple. You persuade her to go to bed with me, and I will help you find out what you want to know.'

145

'What makes you think I have any influence over her? Besides, won't it hurt your pride to have someone argue your case for you? To an old girl friend?'

'Before the war maybe. Now I have no time for pride.'

'She's going to take a lot of persuading.'

'Because you are a lesbian?'

Margaret's laughter ricocheted against the walls.

'Who told you that?'

'Nobody told me. It was obvious when I saw you both before the party. You were embracing her.'

'Oh boy! Give me strength.' They walked on a little way, then Margaret stopped and turned towards Amnon. 'So how do you suggest I persuade her, apart from holding her down while you rape her?'

'If you want your story bad enough, you will think of something.'

'OK. But in return I want the full story behind the shooting of Jane's parents. It's obvious Max was involved, but I want to know if he actually pulled the trigger.'

ARCHIVE FOOTAGE

Jerusalem, Spring

Jane and Naomi were tidying up after the party. Ilan was slumped in a chair, half asleep.

'If you want,' Naomi said, 'we go together to Mount Scopus to find the grave of your parents. I would like to help you.'
Jane smiled. 'Thank you. But I'm not sure I want to go. The past is the past.'

'But your parents, your own mother and father … '

'Which do you mean? My parents, the people who brought me up from when I was three years old are alive and living in England.'

'But, your flesh and blood … '

'Is here,' Jane pinched the flesh in here upper arm, 'standing right in front of you. If you mean the flesh and blood of my mother and father, they are dust near a church wall. It means nothing to me.'

Naomi sighed. 'Why do you reject the past so much? Cut yourself off?' She lowered her voice to a whisper after looking across to where Ilan was dozing. 'You are just like Ilan.'

'Why do you say that? He seems to be obsessed with how he was before he was wounded in the war.'

Naomi nodded slowly. 'Yes, and it is the same thing. You reject, he is a prisoner.'

Jane made a ball of the dishcloth and tossed it in the sink.
'Well, it's too late now.'

***

A few days later, Jane and Margaret were seated at the Steenbeck editing desk of Hebron Films, where Jane worked as a freelance editor. They were looking at some old newsreel footage.

'What I want to do with this sequence is to look at some of the people arrested by the British after the King David hotel was blown up, and try to get some of the survivors to talk about what happened.'

Jane frowned slightly. 'They got blown up surely.'

'I mean the survivors of interrogation by the British. They must have got some rough treatment.'

'Not altogether surprising.' Jane sounded briskly impersonal.

'Maybe not. I expect I'd feel the same if I was personally involved, like you.'

Jane's voice sounded wearied by repetition. 'How many times do I have to say it? I have no personal involvement. It's all old history as far as I'm concerned.' She pressed the start button and the screen flickered. 'Where'd you get all this archive stuff from, anyway?'

'Through a contact of Amnon's.'

'Amnon? He never mentioned it. What's the Israeli deal this time?'

'Israeli deal?'

'It's a joke expression he uses when he wants a big return on a small favour. He seems to be trying very hard to please you all of a sudden. Am I supposed to be jealous?'

'Flattered, according to him.'

Jane pressed the stop button and the screen went blank.

'So, what is the deal? … No, let me guess. He wants to go to bed with you, but wants you to break it to me gently.'

Margaret laughed. 'Nice try, but wrong. The name of the game is not 'break *it* to you gently' but 'break *in* to you gently.'

Jane looked blank.

Margaret went on in a swift singsong, tilting her head from side to side at the end of each sentence. 'He wants your body, I need his footage, so he wants my help.'

'To get me to go to bed with him.'

'Yep.'

'And you agreed?'

'On condition I could tell you the whole story.'

'And if I hold out on you?'

'I don't get to make my documentary, Amnon hangs loose …'

Jane tried hard not to smile.

'… and we don't get to hear who shot your mom and dad.'

'And if I was to say that I don't give a camel's fart about what happened to them … '

'I would say that you were lying.'

Jane paused and drew breath.

'Let me just get this clear in my mind. Amnon fancies me again, although he must have a pretty good idea that I fancy you, while you in turn have rather macabre, even slightly necrophiliac designs on my long dead mother and father, to fulfil which you have agreed to try to persuade me to let Amnon have his evil way etc., etc. That's the moebius-stripped down truth of it, isn't it? A working model lets say.'

'In essence.'

'May I ask what I get out of this strange brew?'

Margaret thought for a moment.

'Pleasure, pain … feeling?'

Jane swivelled her chair round to face Margaret, so fast that the strips of film hanging in the editing bin waiting to be assembled rustled in the breeze.

'That's your prescription, is it? What I need right now to put me right again. Thanks for letting me know. Well I'm sorry, this corner of the triangle won't co-operate. I don't want to be part of you equation of therapeutic convenience. I'll choose my own time to come to terms with my past, if ever, and it sure as hell isn't going to be timed to suit your career structure or Amnon's sex drive.'

Jane swivelled back to face the screen and pressed the fast forward button. History flashed by, emitting bat like squeaks.

'So the deals off,' said Margaret flatly. 'Unless … '

'Unless?' … 'Unless we … sleep together.' … 'We?' … 'You and me.' … 'You don't want to.' … 'No.' … 'But I do.'… 'Yes.' Both women spoke in soft monotones. Jane continued, 'And Amnon does.' … 'Yes.' … 'But I don't.' … 'No.' … 'Just like you don't.' … 'Yes.' … 'But you will, for the sake of your career.' … 'Yes.' … 'And because you think it will help me.' … 'Yes.' … 'And because,' Jane turned slowly to face Margaret,' you … care about me?' … 'Yes.' … 'And desire … me?'

Margaret began to form the word 'no' with her lips. Before she could utter Jane was kissing her full on the mouth and hugging her. There was the sound of flailing celluloid as the end of the film tore loose from its winding spool.

***

Ilan took another totter round the bedroom of the small flat he shared with Naomi. It was in the Shikonim, a collection of buildings hurriedly constructed out of breezeblocks and little else.

Naomi was watching him with growing exasperation.

'You told me the doctors said the plaster should come off this week.' … 'Yes.' … 'So? You've still got it on.' … 'Yes.' … 'The doctors know nothing?' … 'No.' … 'But you still go to see them.' … 'Yes.' … 'Why?' … 'My disability pension.'

Naomi blew through her lips. 'Pwaah! I think you need that disability more than the money. You always talk about it. I never see the money.'

'I'm saving it. For when my son arrives.'

'And if it's a girl?'

'We can go out and get drunk together.'

'Again?'

Ilan stopped and leaned heavily on his stick.

'What else is there to do? We're not war heroes any more. We even have to buy our own drinks again now.'

'Before the war you never needed to drink.'

Ilan gave a disparaging wave of his free hand.

'Tchaah! Before the war, before the war. Before the war was different. I was different. I could walk. Run, even.'

'You could now. There's no need to hobble about on that stupid stick with that filthy bandage wrapped round your foot.'

Ilan looked aggrieved. 'You never wash it.'

'Because, for the last time, you don't need to wear it. It's over.'

Naomi's voice had risen to a near scream. She calmed down and then said, 'Look I'm sick of sitting here arguing with you every night.' She got up and reached for her jacket. 'I'm going to Ta 'amon to see if there's a job for me. Behind the bar maybe.'

Ilan threw his stick on the floor and took a few swift paces to the door to bar her exit, then realising what he had done hobbled back to retrieve the stick and collapsed backwards onto the bed his face contorted in agony.

'I refuse to let you work there,' he shouted at the ceiling. 'I don't want my wife,' he struggled for the right word, 'suckling a bunch of lefties, Arab lovers.'

'And I don't want you sitting around here all day.' Naomi went out slamming the door behind her.

***

At eleven o'clock that evening Margaret and Amnon were sitting in what was becoming their 'usual' corner. There were a couple of fresh lemon teas in front of them. Amnon was helping his drink infuse with the aid of a spoon jabbed repeatedly into the bag of leaves. His actions somewhat undermined the studied casualness with which he spoke.

'So ... What did she say? Did she agree?'

'I'm afraid I can't tell you. You'll have to find out for yourself. You're good at that.'

'But you said ... '

' ... That I would try to persuade her. There's nothing in the small print that says I've got to tell you if I succeeded or not.'

Amnon drained the bowl of the spoon carefully against the inner rim of the glass and placed it in the saucer. His voice was even more controlled.

'So ... how do I know?'

Margaret shrugged as if it was really not her problem.

'Ask her to sleep with you, and see what happens. If she does it probably means I managed to persuade her ... Unless of course she suddenly changed her mind of her own accord.'

Amnon looked steadily at her, his glass poised half way to his lips.

'But you did try.'

As if affirming a vow, Margaret said,' Yes, I did try.'

Amnon took a sip, then put down his glass. He said in resigned tones, 'OK. I have to believe you.'

'Yes you do ... in which case ... ' She opened out her palm towards him. 'You owe me.'

FINK'S

Jerusalem, Spring

That same evening, Max and Lotte had just finished supper at home and were drinking coffee together, accompanied by the sound of the tinned monsoon produced by the dish washer.

Lotte looked up from the letter she was writing to their daughter in America.

'Max, how much do you think that Amnon knows about what you did in '48?'

'Amnon? What should he know? He wasn't around.'

'Oh, Max! Please. Be serious. You know what I mean. He is in intelligence. They still have the files from that time … and he has access to them.'

'How do you know?'

'He told me once. Not directly, but he let slip something that he could only have known from my file.'

Max smiled at her over the top of his reading glasses.

'And what was that? Your other boyfriends? Don't worry, it was a long time ago. I forgive you.'

'Thank you, darling.' Lotte smiled fleetingly, and then grew more serious. She said carefully, 'I was thinking more about your guilty secrets. You always told me that the Daventrys were a mistake … Were they a mistake, Max? I want to know.'

Max started to bluster. 'After twenty years? I don't remember.'

'Oh, yes, you do. I saw how you looked the other evening, at the party … There's something eating you, I can feel it. Tell me. What is it?'

Max folded his paper and put it to one side.

'Nothing … something … everything … nothing.' He paused for thought, then continued, 'It was just something about Ilan's attitude that made me realise that he and I were fighting for two different countries … No, not that … two

153

different times. A future and a past. Without establishing the state of Israel, we would have had no future, but, only twenty years on, this same state begins to turn towards the past. To yearn for the trappings of imperialism … '

'Rubbish!' Lotte broke in vehemently,' We fought the Six Day War to survive, not to set up our own Middle Eastern Raj, or, forgive me for saying it, to satisfy our need for Lebensraum.'

'That's not how the PLO would see it.'

'That's their business.' Lotte adopted a gently teasing tone. 'What's the matter with you, Liebchen? You're getting soft in your old age. Where's the Max I used to smuggle weapons for in the old days? Hot Shot Maxie, lounging in the alleyway … The British soldiers too polite to search a lady … I felt sorry for those two, him with his stick and dirty bandage. He didn't seem to know what he was doing or what he was fighting for. Not like you … us.'

Max sounded tired and full of doubt.

'You knew? What did you know? Tell me.'

Lotte resumed writing her letter and spoke crossly.

'Max, you are being ridiculous now. It was obvious.' She signed the bottom of the sheet and collecting the pages together, folded them to fit the envelope.

'A homeland for the victims of persecution.'

She licked the triangular flap of the envelope and then folded it down, securing it with a series of short sweeps with the side of her clenched fist finishing with a couple of blows at the apex of the triangle for good measure.

'What's got into you? This is kindergarten stuff.' She got up and put the letter on the sideboard for posting the next morning.

'Come on. It's no good sitting here brooding. Let's go to Fink's. We haven't been there for such a long time.' She began sorting through the coats on the hat stand for something to put on.

Max hadn't moved. 'It's getting late, Lottchen. Another night maybe. I don't feel like it tonight.'

Lotte turned reluctantly back to the table and sat down.

'OK, but won't you at least tell me what's wrong?'

There was a brooding silence, and then Max said,

'They didn't tell me that the Daventrys had a little daughter.'

'Would that have stopped you?'

'At the time, no. But it's made me stop to think now.'

'And?'

'I am beginning to wonder what else they didn't tell me. There was something strange about the whole business. The way they sent the orders. Through you, at the very last moment, but with a top priority coding so that I didn't hesitate.' Max lit up a cigar. 'The way there was almost nothing in the Post about it. Just two lines, like a traffic accident ... Even the way they looked at me as I approached. Just a glance, and only full attention as the bullets entered ... He fell first, I remember, but he held her round the knees for a moment, as if he was trying to shield her.' Max was forced to chuckle at the black absurdity of the picture. 'Not much use ... I was aiming a little higher. Then she fell on top of him, and they both lay in a heap against the wall ... '

'And then you came running past me and slipped the gun into my bag.'

' And then, nothing. Silence. As if I had made a big mistake. No contact. No debriefing. I was just dropped from the rota. Wiped off. Nobody ever told me why.'

Lotte made to say something, but then thought better of it.

As if reading her thoughts, Max went on,

'Oh, sure, I was very small fry. Just like the Daventrys. Why bother with two minor civil servants and just another gunman.' Max leaned across to an ashtray and tapped the end off his cigar. 'But then again, it must have taken some effort to hush it up. Even just to raise a finger to cross me off the list ... Why did they think I was worth it?'

155

'Maybe Amnon can find out for you. Why don't you ask him?'

'Why should he want to help me?'

'If he won't do it for you, he'll do it for Jane, maybe.'

'And lead her straight to me, if she doesn't suspect already.'

'She may suspect that you pulled the trigger, but if even you don't know the full reason why, how can she put all the blame on you?'

Max gave a snort of amusement,

'She's an odd girl. She seems to lack any curiosity about the past. Most people would have jumped on what I said the other evening. As that other girl did. Jane just let it drop, backed away. However, in order for me to purge my guilt and satisfy my curiosity, Amnon needs to rouse and satisfy Jane's curiosity about why her parents were killed. A complicated and dangerous game.'

Lotte smiled, 'Just like old times?'

'That wasn't a game.'

'Not for us, maybe.'

Suddenly Max stubbed out his cigar, half consumed, and stood up.

'I've changed my mind. Let's go and see who's around at Fink's.'

'That's my Hot Shot.'

'In that case, you'd better bring your bag.'

***

In Fink's Bar the clientele tended towards the '48 generation, apart from Amnon and Jane who were sitting at one of the tables.

'Margaret explained everything to you?' Amnon asked.

'Yes, the whole deal. All the Israeli gears.'

'And what did you say?'

Jane shook her head.' I can't tell you that, but you'll know when, if, the time comes.'

'But you did reach a decision?'

'Oh, yes. I know my place, which cog in the machine I represent.'

'But when the motor gets in gear, which way are you going to turn?'

'I really can't say. I'm not a mechanic. All I can say is that I will turn, revolve. Against which other cog and whether clockwise or anti-clockwise I can't predict.'

'That all depends on the drive wheel. Me.'

'Don't be so sure.' As she spoke Jane saw Max and Lotte enter. They looked round, saw that the only space was at Jane and Amnon's table, and, after a brief discussion, made their way over.

'Hello again,' said Lotte. 'We didn't expect to find you in this old people's home. May we join you?'

Amnon smiled. 'Sure, please do.'

The waiter, who looked like a black olive on legs, came over and Max ordered two drinks. He spoke in Hebrew.

Jane said to Lotte, 'Amnon said he wanted a change from Ta'amon, so we ended up here.'

'I expect you wanted a break from keeping an eye on things, eh, Amnon?' said Max.

'What does he mean?' asked Jane.

'I'll explain later,' said Amnon hurriedly.

The waiter returned with two drinks on a tray and set down on each in front of Max and Lotte.

'One bloody Mary, one Marguerita.'

Max thanked him.

Jane looked disappointed.

'Is that what you call them. We were in the Puss-Puss the other night and Amnon assured me that all drinks were named after distinguished Israelis. You know Dayan, Ben Gurion. We were getting quite sloshed on Triple Goldas at the time.'

Max gave Amnon a sour look.

'I think Amnon must have been deceiving you. He is quite good at that. Most professional about it you could say.'

'Just making sure that the achievements of your generation are not forgotten,' Amnon said with icy politeness.

Jane leaned across the table to Lotte.

'This is all beyond me. Especially when they start talking Hebrew.'

Lotte gave he a shrewd smile,

'Maybe that is just as well.'

'How do you mean?'

'What they have to say may upset you. Remind you of what happened here when you were a little girl.'

Jane waved a dismissive hand. 'Oh, that. Doesn't bother me a bit. It's a closed book. They're just two lines in the stop press. Even got the names wrong. My mother keeps the clipping in her recipe book. I have absolutely no feelings one way or another about them.'

Jane gulped down the rest of her drink as Lotte smiled to herself.

Max and Amnon were deep in conversation in Hebrew.

'I want you to look up the files on them,' Max was saying, 'and find out for me who wanted them killed, and why.'

Amnon nodded, 'All right, but on one condition. That you agree to speak, on camera, to Margaret about what happened.'

Jane interrupted with a beaming smile.

'Margaret. There's a word I'm familiar with. What's she doing in '48.'

Reverting to English, Amnon replied, 'For her I think it is strictly business. She's just here to do a job. Somebody picks a target for her and she pulls the trigger.'

Lotte and Max exchange glances.

Jane said excitedly,

'No, you're quite wrong. She does it because she believes that people should know the facts about what went on. Unless the viewer knows as much as possible about the reasons behind certain actions, the motives of those involved, it reduces everything to random chance, and people to mindless automata, victims and executioners alike. The behaviour of robots is entirely uninteresting.'

'You despise your mother and father for being victims of chance?' Lotte asked.

'No, as I said, they arouse no emotion whatever in me.'

Max had been listening intently to this last interchange. As Jane finished speaking, he leaned across the table, shook Amnon by the hand, and said in Hebrew,

'For the sake of the victims and the executioner, it's a deal.'

Although she hadn't understood what Max had said, Jane was pleased at this rapprochement between the two men.

'That looked hopeful. If anybody's about to order another round, I'll have a Moses-in-the-Bullrushes.'

***

The following afternoon, Margaret was sitting alone at a table in Ta'amon making notes. The barman brought her another lemon tea and handed her a fold of paper.

'Someone left this for you,' he said in English.

'For me? Who was it?'

The barman shook his head and walked off.

Margaret opened out the paper and read,
' I HAVE MAXIMUM INFORMATION. MEET ME BY THE WINDMILL AT NINE. AMNON.' She looked baffled, then with a shrug she put the note in her pocket, and went on writing.

After a while she looked up at the clock and saw it was half past eight. She pondered for a moment and then came to a decision. Gathering her belongings together, she went over to the bar and paid for her drinks.

'Do you know of a windmill around these parts.'

'Sure, out on the Bethlehem road. About twenty minutes walk.'

IN COLD BLOOD AND GOOD FAITH

Jerusalem, Spring

Late next morning Jane was alone, at a loose end. 'Strange Brew' played softly. She wandered from room to room, picking things up and then putting them down again. She walked over to the mirror and stared into it for a long time, then turned and looked at the dining room table.

On impulse, she wandered over to it and tipped the chairs so that the backs rested on the table rim, covered by the edges of the tablecloth. She stood back to look, her head to one side. Then, with a sudden inspired burst of energy, she ran into the bedroom and came back with the carpet bundled in her arms and draped round her head and shoulders like some huge shawl. This she laid over the whole structure. She paused again, head cocked. Quite clear now, she ran back into the bedroom and returned with a blanket and a couple of pillows, and in a crouching run, as if under sniper fire, disappeared under the table.

After the scuffling sounds of nesting there was a long silence.

A few moments later there was a tentative ring on the doorbell, scarcely audible above the record player. Then another ring, louder this time.

From within her hovel Jane shouted,
'Who is it?'
'It is me. Naomi.' Naomi walked in and looked around the room. There was silence. After waiting for a while she approached the croft and bent down.
'Hello?'
There was a short pause, and then Jane scrambled out, saw Naomi, made as if to dismantle the structure, realised it was too late, and tried to hide her embarrassment with a great show of

turning down the record player. Having done this she turned, trying to smooth down her hair as she did so.

'I'm afraid the place is in a bit of a mess.' As she became less flustered, she saw that Naomi's eyes were red and her left cheek and upper lip were swollen. 'My God! What's happened to you? Are you all right? Who did that to you?' Jane disentangled a couple of chairs from her temporary edifice and set them side-by-side on the bare floor. 'Come and sit down.'

Naomi did so, and began to cry.

'It was Ilan. I told him I was leaving and he beat me.'

'Leaving him? Why?'

'He won't let me have any freedom. Won't let me out of the house. Ever since the war, he's changed. I thought the baby would make things better but they are worse. He's twice as jealous now. I can't stand it any longer. So this evening I told him I didn't want to have the baby any more and he went crazy. I'm frightened to go back home.'

Jane put a hand on her shoulder.

'I'm sure when he's had a chance to calm down, he'll be OK. Why don't you stay here for a while until things get sorted out?'

'You are very kind. But I will never go back to him. It is over.'

Suddenly there was a thunderous knocking on the outside door, followed by a roar of 'Naomi!'

Naomi leapt to her feet with a terrified squeak and whispered, 'It's Ilan. Save me.'

Jane pointed to the shack and said,

'You'll have to hide in there, while I try to calm him down.'

Gripped by panic, Naomi scrambled inside and Jane closed the two chairs behind her. As she walked to the door the thunder was interspersed with the sharper crack of wood on wood.

'N-A-O-M-I-I-I!'

Jane opened the door to find Ilan, his arms raised in front of him, the fist and the walking stick poised for another assault.

When he saw Jane he lowered both arms and leaned heavily on the stick, thrusting the grubby bandage forward for greater effect.

'I want to speak with my wife.'

'I'm afraid she's not here.'

Ilan pushed past her and hobbled into the dining room. On seeing the bunker, he looked slightly taken aback and looked slowly round the rest of the room.

He rounded on Jane. 'Where is she? I have searched many Arab houses before so it is better you tell me before I start work.'

'And I think it would be better for you not to threaten me,' said Jane quietly.

Suddenly, from within the refuge there came a high-pitched stream of very angry sounding Hebrew. For the next few minutes Jane had to content herself, as so often, with catching the general drift.

'Ilan, please go away. It's too late. I'm leaving you.'

'You do not take my son. You have no right. I will kill you if you do. You have no right.'

'Big Man! You almost did, already. You're lucky the baby wasn't harmed.'

'Because you did not obey me. I have no respect in my house. You do what you like, when you like.'

During this interchange, Ilan was circling the lean-to shouting down into it, not quite sure where Naomi was located within. This served to detract somewhat from his patriarchal dignity.

Despite her amusement, Jane remained watchful, in case she was misreading the situation.

'All this talk about War Heroes. It's gone to your head. Who do you think you are?' Naomi shrieked, still in Hebrew.

Ilan replied in kind, but slowly and, it seemed to Jane, a hint of menace.

'I am going to count to five. If you are not out by then, I'm coming in to get you. One . . . two . . . three . . . four . . . '

'Don't you dare!' Naomi's tone had changed from terror to indignation.

'FIVE!' Ilan threw down his stick and scrambled into the temporary dwelling. The sound of a shrieking rough and tumble prompted Jane to follow, but just as she was about to do so the rhythm changed to that of a typical 'Yes, you did ... no, I didn't' argument.

Jane hovered anxiously for a while, then relaxed.

After a while she decided to go for a walk, left the house and strode purposefully off.

***

Amnon stood in the doorway of the half empty Ta'amon and looked around anxiously.

'Have you seen the black American girl in here this evening?' he called to the man behind the bar.

'She left a little while ago. Said something about the Windmill.'

***

Margaret began to fidget. Could there be another Windmill? A figure limped towards her in the dark.

'Where the hell have you been?' Her relief put an angry edge on her words.

'We said Ta'amon, I believe.'

'I was there until I got your note asking to meet me here ... alone. Very cloak and dagger.'

'What note are you talking about?'

Margaret handed him the fold of paper.

'What does it say?'

'Something like 'Meet me at the Windmill. I've got maximum information.'

164

'You are right. It is like a spy film. But I did not write it.'
'So what's going on?'
'I don't know.'
'But I'm sure you'll find out … Talking of which what is the
latest on Max?'
'I can't tell you yet.'
'The small print on the deal. I forgot. Remind me again.
What's the problem?'
'The problem is that neither of us knows for sure if the other
can deliver. We must arrange to hand over where everything is
clear.'
'So what do you suggest?'

***

At the turning point of one of her favourite walks, Jane froze.
'Everything is clear.' It sounded like Amnon.
'So what do you suggest?' That was unmistakably Margaret's
voice.
She turned softly (thank God for rope soled shoes) and ran
towards home.
As she turned a corner a figure came hurrying towards her,
head down and covered with a scarf. Jane couldn't stop herself
colliding with what felt like a woman. The figure dropped a
bag on the ground, spilling the contents. Jane bent down to help
retrieve them and was astonished to see that they included a
handgun. She looked into the face of the woman crouched next
to her.
'Lotte! What are you doing here? And what's this?' Jane held
out the gun for her to inspect.
Lotte laughed.
'That's just a toy. It belongs to my little grandson. He's crazy
about playing soldiers. It must have slipped into my bag by
accident. You poor girl. All alone in the dark with Lotte

Luger.' She laughed again. 'So what brings you out here, if I may ask?'

'I just wanted a breath of fresh air … Margaret and Amnon are over by the Windmill. Shall we join them?'

'OK.' Lotte sounded totally indifferent at the prospect.

As they approached the Windmill, Jane heard Margaret say wearily,

'Yes, for the last time, it's a deal.' She could see them shaking hands.

'Hi.' Amnon and Margaret turned, looking surprised and puzzled in equal measure. 'Everything settled,' Jane went on.

'Just tying up a few loose ends,' said Margaret.

'That's good. I expect you'll be keeping me informed.'

'Better than that.' Margaret paused for dramatic effect. 'We want to borrow your house.'

'What's mine is yours, as you know.'

Margaret continued, 'And we'd like to borrow your husband, Lotte. Just for tonight.'

***

Max and Lotte arrived just after midnight, just as the camera crew had finished setting up.

Max entered the room first, with Lotte, clutching her handbag, walking a couple of paces behind him, body guard style, her eyes scanning the room. He made straight for the chair opposite the one Margaret was sitting in. Behind her were Amnon and Jane, out of shot, sitting slightly apart. Having checked that the camera was turning over and the sound rolling, Margaret spoke.

'Max Linden, in the period leading up to the '48 war, you were, I believe, the appointed executioner for one of the main groups engaged in the struggle against the British to establish a Jewish homeland in what was then Palestine.'

Max hunched forward, his elbows on the arm of the chair.

'I preferred to think of myself as a soldier, not an executioner. A specialist soldier. But yes, that was my business at the time.'

'And, at the time, you had no doubts about the morality of what you were doing?'

'No, because there was always logic behind it, always strategy, always reason.' Max pursed his lips and made as if to remove some fragment of cigar leaf from his lower lip.

'Always logic? Always reason?' Margaret laid heavy emphasis on 'always'.

'Sure, as far as our own operations went. Some of the other groups were maybe not so careful.'

'And what was the logic, what was the strategy, what was the reason,' Margaret's voice had fallen in to a singsong. Then she paused. 'Behind the killings of the Daventrys.'

Sounding as if he had decided against a particular item on the menu, Max said,

'I have no information about that.'

'But you were involved?'

Jane found herself biting hard into her lower lip.

'I pulled the trigger, yes.'

'But perhaps, just this once, without logic, strategy or reason?'

Max appeared to be waving away an invisible gnat.

'There was no time to explain. I did it in good faith.'

'That must have been a comfort to the Daventrys. To be murdered in cold blood and killed in good faith. This good faith was enough to convince you that they deserved to die. That they were sufficient of a threat to the birth of the state of Israel to be … exterminated … at random.'

'Not at random. It was strategically necessary.'

There was a long pause during which Max stared unblinkingly at Margaret before searching his breast pocket in vain for a cigar, and then easing back in his seat.

'Despite your almost blind faith in the correctness of your actions, would it interest you to know that history is on your side?' Max's jaw line sagged a millimetre. 'According to our latest research.'

Jane glanced swiftly at Amnon, who remained impassive. Lotte took a firmer grip on her handbag, slid her hand inside and then brought it slowly out again … empty.

Max looked straight at Jane, as he said,

'So, these were no robots, the Daventrys.'

'Far from it,' said Margaret. 'They were quite a pair, these innocent bystanders. Very active, in fact. Very 'intelligent' you could say. Quite important fish in a very complicated little pond.'

Max gave a 'so what's new' shrug.

'A lot of my 'clients' worked for British intelligence.' 'According to the files, there was more to it than that. The Daventrys were double agents.'

Max graciously conceded a point.

'Which once again destroys the logic … '

'Until,' Margaret said slowly, 'we discovered that they were about to become triple agents. Or, worse, defect to the Palestinian cause.'

For the first time Max looked wholly involved.

'Which no one told me. 'He looked at Lotte. 'I don't understand.'

'From the notes in your file,' Margaret went on,' it looks as though your controllers were afraid that you might not go through with it once you discovered that your targets were as idealistic as you were, with minds of their own. Not simply cogs in the machine of British imperialism.'

Max struggled to regain his composure.

'Sure, I had doubts occasionally. But I never voiced them. Never told any one.'

Lotte spoke.

'You told me, Max.'

Max's mouth opened and closed. There was silence except for the faint whirr of the recording devices. Finally Max whispered,

'And you never told me?'

He rested his face in his hand. The cameraman raised an eyebrow questioningly at Margaret and she motioned to him to keep filming. Grief was very private, but she knew it often made for compelling television.

'What would have been the point? Haven't we been happy together?'

Max went on as if he hadn't heard her.

'For twenty years you allowed me to think that I had committed a senseless act of destruction, kept me in ignorance of the full meaning of my actions and you call that being happy together? What gave you the right?'

Lotte seemed to be reciting something.

'We thought it was for the best. After all, it helped us win the war.'

Max's eyes were brimming.

'And destroyed my peace of mind.'

STRAY SHOTS

Jerusalem, Spring

'It was easier somehow to write them off when I thought they
were victims of chance. It made them sort of two dimensional
cardboard cut-outs; Everyman and Wife. Nothing to do with
me. Me, with my hopes and fears and changes. Intentions. Now
it's harder for me, having glimpsed them as people destroyed
by actions for which they took full responsibility. Full
responsibility. I wonder if I really know what I've been doing
all this time. The behaviour of a robot ... '

Jane glanced across at Amnon, lying in bed beside her. He
reached to the bedside chair and took out a packet of cigarettes
from his jacket pocket. He searched again but came out empty
handed.

He turned to Jane.

'Have you any matches?'

'I don't smoke ... Oh, wait a minute. I'll see if there are any in
Lotte's bag. Jane reached down beside the bed and pulled the
bag onto her lap. After rummaging in it she pulled out the gun.

'Sorry, kid, no matches.' On impulse she trained the gun on
him. 'Anyway, why smoke yourself to death when you can do
it the easy way?' She pulled the trigger. Silence.' Where's the
safety catch on this?'

Amnon smiled indulgently and rolled over to take a closer
look. As he did so, his expression changed. He lunged for
Jane's hand, knocking the gun from her grasp. As it hit the
ground there was a loud explosion and the sound of breaking
glass. Jane looked up to see that the full-length mirror on the
opposite wall had gone blind.

'My God, Amnon, I could have killed you.'

'Or been killed.'

'She said it was a toy. Belonged to her grandson.'

Amnon was pulling on his clothes, like a fighter pilot scrambling to a long awaited call.

'When did she tell you this?'

'Yesterday evening. I bumped into her -literally- while I was out walking near the Windmill. Just before I met you and Margaret. Honestly, Amnon, I had absolutely no idea.'

Amnon paused in the doorway,

'Wait here till I get back. Don't let anyone in.'

***

In the living room of Max and Lotte's house, the table was strewn with the debris of the all night heart-to-heart; coffee cups, ashtrays, and an almost empty bottle of brandy.

Max moved his head from side to side in a slow mixture of disbelief and fatigue.

'I still don't understand why you left your handbag there, Lottchen. You never used to be so careless.'

Lotte sighed and patted Max's hand across the table.

'Maybe not so careless. It's getting late. I wanted things settled.'

'Late? For what?'

'Us ... The country.' She shook her head. 'I don't know. They used to be the same. But now.'

Max patted her hand.

'Come on,' he said gently. 'They're not all like Ilan. Our son would have been different. We would have made sure of that.'

'Perhaps. But look at Amnon. Mother and father life long socialists, the backbone of the kibbutz movement, and now he just screws around, eager for the next bandwagon.' She laughed softly. 'After this evening he'll be calling himself a television director, you'll see.'

There was a ring at the front door. Max and Lotte looked at each other in surprise and then Max went to open the door. He found Amnon, flanked by two armed policemen.

171

'How can I help you, gentlemen?'

'I have come to speak to your wife,' Amnon said.

'May I ask, on what authority?'

Amnon said nothing, but merely slid a corner of blue plastic into view from his breast pocket.

With the satisfaction of a crossword puzzler solving an infuriatingly elusive clue, Max said.

'So that's who you are. You'd better come in. You won't need your private army.'

Amnon motioned to the two policemen to go back to the car. He and Max walked through to the living room.

'Hello, Amnon, I wondered if it would be you.' Lotte sounded pleased with herself.

Amnon made no reply, but strode to the table and placed the gun upon it. Then with a slight bow and a headwaiter's sweep of the arms he said,

'Please sit down.'

***

Jane froze. There was another knock. Louder this time. Throwing on her dressing gown Jane tiptoed clear of the cold stone and shouted through the door,

'Who's there?'

'Margaret. Can you let me in?'

The door, as usual, stuck slightly then shuddered open.

'What's up?'

'You tell me. Amnon just called to say you needed looking after. Didn't have time to explain. Just told me to go round 'now' to see you.' They both walked into the dining room.

'Everything all right?'

Jane nodded. 'Fine, apart from nearly shooting him dead about half an hour ago.'

'What!'

'Look, I'll show you the bullet hole.'

Jane led Margaret into the bedroom and pointed to the mirror.
'Jeeezus! What happened ... He didn't try to rape you?'
Jane slipped her feet into her backless slippers.
'No. Nothing like that. Under the terms of our domino effect agreement, we had just spent a not unpleasant night together.'
Margaret's face became a gargoyle of inquisitive surprise.
'Since you struggle not to ask, he was rather sweet actually; apologetic and decisive at all the appropriate moments ... You should give him a whirl.'
'So why did you try to kill him?'

***

Lotte glanced at the scrap of paper and handed it back to Amnon.
'Yes, I sent it to her. I wanted to get her on her own.'
'To shoot her?'
'That's Max's department.' Lotte smiled at her husband.' I just wanted to warn her off. I was going to wave it at her if she was slow about agreeing. I had no idea it was loaded.'
'You really expect me to believe this?,' said Amnon wearily.
'Believe what you like. It's true. Tell him, Max.'
Max didn't reply immediately, and then turned to Amnon, and said,
'Will you give us five minutes alone? I think I have a solution to all this.'
'OK, but no longer.'
Amnon walked from the room and down to his car where the two policemen were waiting. Instead of joining them in the car he leaned against the bonnet and, putting his hands in his pockets, gazed at the lighted window of the room he had just left.

***

173

Margaret poured herself another coffee.

'So, until Lord Amnon sounds the all clear, what do we do? Play cards? Dominoes . . . . Talking of which, it's your turn.'

Jane looked blank.

'For what?'

'Getting your part of the deal. You know, having your wicked way with me.'

'Oh, yes, I suppose it must be.' Jane sounded far from overjoyed.

'I'm so flattered by the barely suppressed eagerness in your tone.'

Jane laughed,

'I'm sorry. It's nothing personal, I promise.'

'I'm sure there's a compliment in there somewhere if I look hard enough.'

'It's just that you happened to be there when I came out of the deep freeze. Rather ironic in view of the fact that I blamed you for being on ice in the first place. It was after John told me about you and him having an affair. That day I lost my temper with you was the first time I'd allowed myself to feel anything deeply for years. I cut myself dead, short-circuited myself. Just gave the baby away.'

'Baby?'

'Yes. Didn't he tell you? It was born shortly after John left me. I just gave it away. Never even laid eyes on it. Didn't want to see it or look at it. Just left the hospital empty handed.' Jane had curled her upper lip under her teeth. After a pause she went on.' Blamed you for that of course. Anyone but myself. I just didn't realise that I was part of the story too. Not only that, I was actually one of the tellers of the tale. Not simply the robot victim. Any more than my mother and father were.' Jane smiled at Margaret. 'In fact, I'm having to adjust to the idea that I come from a long line of flesh and blood humans. It's been quite a shock.' Margaret smiled, but did not speak.' One thing I have decided is that it is up to me to stop being a spare cog, a guest in the machine as Koestler almost put it, and be a driving force somewhere, start turning under my own power. So I'm going back to England to get stuck in. I may not always understand what's going on, but at least I'll speak the language. Who knows, I might even learn to take the blame from time to time.'

Margaret leaned over and patted her on the cheek.

'Don't be too hard on yourself. Hell hath no fury like a woman spitting in the mirror.' Margaret pulled out strands of her hair to look like Medusa after having been dragged through a hedge backwards and, sticking her tongue out while grimacing horribly, assumed the look of an avenging gargoyle. Both she and Jane rolled around in fits of laughter.

***

Bearhug had gained fleeting control of the Puss-Puss club turntable and 'Sunshine of Your Love' was playing a sufficient level to qualify as background music. The doors swung open and shut. This time there was no potted biography from Amnon. He was too busy telling Jane and Margaret what had happened that evening.

'We waited for about five minutes, and then there was a single shot. It is very sad.'

As he spoke, the door pushed open, slowly as if by an invalid. Lotte pushed her way slowly into view, resting on a stick, her left foot swathed on a huge white bandage. She was followed by Max, looking decidedly embarrassed.

Jane smiled across at Amnon.

'It looks like someone missed.'

Amnon, his story scattered to the winds, stared at them open mouthed.

BEARHUG

Jerusalem, Spring

' ... so that's why everybody calls you Bearhug,' said Jane, sipping her second lemon tea of the evening in Ta'amon.

Bearhug grinned yet another sheepish grin and, little finger cocked, finished the last of his coffee.

'You mean I really do all that. I can't believe it. Have I hurt any body?'

'Only national pride now and again, when you go on about the music they play in Puss-Puss. How awful it is and why don't they listen to some good music for a change.'

A large bearded man sitting within earshot at the next table started singing the opening guitar riff to 'Sunshine of your Love' and the tune was taken up by the rest of the cafe. Everyone started laughing and pointing at Bearhug. He tried to brazen it out by raising his arms in a victory salute and shouting,

'Thank you, fans.' Then to Jane, 'God! How embarrassing. I think it's time I went home. To England.'

As he spoke Jane felt a wave of homesickness. She felt that she had absolutely no reason to stay in this enigmatic little town a minute longer. Despite the fact that all the mystery surrounding her parents' death had been cleared up, she felt just as much in the dark as before. The clearer everything became, the more she puzzled over it.

On impulse she said,

'Can I come with you?'

Bearhug looked very startled.

'But of course. I'm afraid you'll have to pay your own fare though. Because I'm still sitting on the head of salaries desk, literally, trying to get my back pay for the last three months.

What makes you want to go all of a sudden? Not just my irresistibly bad behaviour, I imagine.'

Jane smiled,

'No. I can live without that. I just want someone to travel home with.'

'Oh, I see.'

'Also, there are things I've seen here that I want to protest about, but it's not my place to do so.'

'For example?'

'Oh, I can't say. Just something I saw in the market that upset me. There was a bunch of Arabs standing in the back of a truck. Some soldiers were giving them a hard time.'

Despite the fact that they were sitting in a radical hotbed, Jane felt obliged to lower her voice.

'Beating them up you mean?' Bearhug spoke normally. 'Something like that.' Jane, not wanting to say any more, got up to pay the bill.

'What about Amnon? Can't he help you out? I'm sure he's got enough connections.'

'He's got the connections all right. I just don't think he'll be able to help me when it comes to the crunch.'

1977

THE BOTTOM LINE

Shortly after they had been introduced,
their brief acquaintance having ripened to
extreme intimacy with surreal speed, a
pretty young doctor had her finger stuck
firmly up his arse. Having withdrawn, she
was happy to let him know that it was, as
he had hoped, only piles and that she
would make him an appointment to see the
gut surgeon. She thought that he would
either be injected or that there would be
little bands tied round each pile so that
they would wither and die. This second
option sounded very tricky to him, and he
hoped privately that it would not prove
necessary.

As they rode home in the taxi he was
relieved enough to be making bad jokes
about stigmata (inappropriate
manifestations of) and treats for vampire
bats. His wife was kind enough to humour
the patient.

So began his brief career as a woman. He
decided that the best solution, pending
extremely minor (he hoped) surgery was to
treat the whole thing as a heavy period.
Which explained why super STs came into
his life. Because of certain anatomical
differences, he wore them back to front.

It so happened that they turned out to be
unnecessary, but were a great aid to his
peace of mind nonetheless.

He was a little late for his appointment
for the procedure (as the doctor had put
it) because of an unofficial tube strike,

which had a knock on effect on the rest of London traffic. The waiting room was packed, and so, having picked out one of the less dog-eared glossies, all of which were dedicated to topics that were of absolutely no interest to him he settled down for the usual two-hour wait.

Hardly had he done so than his name was called and he was ushered into a room and told to take the bottom half of his clothes off. As he did so he noticed, half way up on the wall opposite the couch the skid marks left by a small and obviously very grubby hand.

While he was wondering how these marks got there, other than through a frenzied attempt to escape during the course of a particular procedure, a nurse wheeled in a trolley load of instruments and then, without looking at or speaking to him, went out again.

He gave the equipment a brief glance. He saw an anonymous black box, with a tube running out of it, and (here was the bad news) some metal instruments, snub nosed and polished thorough much use, which were an ideal basis for any Dyno-Rod fantasies that he might wish to construct. He preferred not to, and turned his back on it all.

After a couple of minutes, Mr B, The Surgeon, a short humourless looking Greek Cypriot, entered, followed by a rather embarrassed looking man of similar appearance, whom he did not bother to introduce. Mr B posed a few cursory

questions and then, having asked him to
lie on his side, got stuck in.

The humiliation he had wished to avoid in
Selfridges was as nothing compared with
the hundred carat Real Thing. Pausing only
to leave the room to discuss an upcoming
colon section (much more interesting) with
a colleague who came in just as he had
begun his examination, Mr B spent half an
hour completely rewriting The Golden
Treasury of Embarrassment. He decided that
he would be able to draw comfort from it
the next time he passed the port the wrong
way round the table.

Matters were made worse by the fact that
he could not see what was going on, and so
had to rely on Mr B's extremely terse and
decidedly grudging admissions of what he
was up to.

'I'm just going to have a look around,'
meant, presumably, that he was shoving in
the requisite footage of flexible tubing
and reading information from some kind of
screen on the enigmatic black box.

Later on, there was a certain amount of
unexplained pushing and shoving followed
by the growing certainty that, either
through the effect of fear on his own
internal organs or because Mr B. was
simply (simply!) pumping air into him from
outside, he was about to fart.

Having said a little earlier, through
gritted teeth, that he was afraid he
wasn't being very brave, he now found
himself delivering a short address to his
little congregation on the theme of

'Breaking Wind'. He wondered if Mr B. was sufficiently versed in English euphemisms to understand what he was implying, and hoped that the nurse would translate for him if he wasn't.

Mr B. replied immediately to the effect that it would be no problem if his forecast should proved correct, so he relaxed into the old routine of grunting through the side of my mouth as nonchalantly as he could. This moved the nurse to put her hand briefly on his shoulder, which he felt sure was disobeying orders, but for which I felt grateful nonetheless.

After another small eternity of insertions and extractions, mysterious gushings of warm liquid (his entire lower bowel disintegrating, perhaps?) and the much heralded ill wind, Mr B. said,

'We have a new treatment now. With heat. You will not feel any pain.'

This sounded like an order it would be unwise for him to disobey, so he maintained radio silence for the final round.

The probing was now accompanied by bursts of low heat, like having his rectum burnished with a forty-watt bulb. The occasional sharp pinprick meant, he assumed, one less haemorrhoid to worry about.

Suddenly it was over, and Mr B was telling him to come back in six weeks, having failed to crack a smile at his would be cheerily ingratiating stories of

182

having had to appropriate his wife's
sanitary towels (Ha Ha?).
 He was left alone to get slowly dressed,
with the feeling of having experienced the
closest thing to male rape outside
Pentonville Prison.

INHUMAN RESOURCES

London, Spring

At the far end of the Library sat Mr Bailey, the longest serving supply teacher in London, if not the world. After twenty-five years he had been thinking of writing his autobiography 'Between the Covers,' a play on the main job of a supply teacher, to stand in for an absent staff member, and a homage to his ruling passion, cricket. A passion he indulged when permitted by his duties as general secretary and prime bond forger of the links between the Caribbean island where he was born and the tattered remnants of the Bloomsbury set. Not the first eleven, but some quite useful all-rounders of the 'My Father knew E. M. Forster' variety.

At the other end of the Library sat Mrs Booklet, the longest serving School Librarian in London, sipping a large gin and tonic. Less of a sun downer (it being scarcely nine in the morning) than a propper upper, to help her face, after twenty three years, up to a hundred and five girls in the library every break time.

A good many of these girls had been inspired to use the library by Mr. Fumble, The Magician. This was now his professional name, but he had galvanised them last term by being a brilliant History teacher called Mr Keep, who sent girls down to do real research of the sort the Librarian had despaired of seeing again. Mr Fumble had made Mr Keep disappear at half term, saying that, although he loved the actual teaching, all the other hassle just wasn't worth it.

In the next room stood a queue of teachers waiting to use the heavy-duty photocopier. On the door of the room was taped a large notice which read,

'YES - The photocopier has broken down.

YES - We have called the engineer.

NO - We don't know when it will be working again.'

Despite this, each new member of the queue asked the person ahead of them,

'Has the photocopier broken down?'

Each time the question was raised the engineer, who was crouched out of sight, with most of the machine's guts strewn about him on the floor, said, with increasing weariness,

'Be another ten minutes.'

At the head of the queue, the runner up for this year's Headless Chicken Award (sponsored and judged by the Media Resources Officer's department and always a close decision), suddenly cracked.

'You said that ten minutes ago. Honestly! This is ridiculous. I've got a class waiting.'

She clutched her files and folders closer to her and scurried out of the room. The queue shuffled forward a couple of feet.

As it did so, the pips went and the Tannoy said,

'Here are the Taddoy announcebents.' The speaker, one of the deputy heads, had absolutely nil microphone technique. Obviously the result of a youth misspent in the study carrel without ever once playing in a rock'n'roll band. His voice was a high wind that blurred and blustered the words.

'Girss are rebinded that they are in year groupss thiss year, sso, instebb of going to their housse bassess after assebbly could they pleass go to their year bassess. Thesse will for the time being be the ssame ass their housse basses were lasst terb.

Girss are orsso rebinded that the film of 'Greasse' will be sshown during lunch break in the lowere assebbly hall. There will be a ten pee entrance fee wissh will go to the Bangladessh Flood Relief Fund.'

The MRO turned to his AV technician with a look of mournful triumph.

'Thought so. Breaking the law again. I've told them a thousand times. For the purposes of the Copyright Law schools constitute a public place. And as for charging an entrance fee!'

He tucked a box of electronic stencils under his arm and retreated to his office. Debbie, the AV technician, a girl of about eighteen, looked up from her drawing board where she was putting the finishing touches to a worksheet. She was about to say something but the MRO's office door closed before she was able to. Instead, she turned round and shrugged at the teachers in what remained of the queue. One of them raised an eyebrow.

'We have been warned,' he said in mock awe, and then came over to the drawing board.

'That's nice. All your own work?'

'Oh no. I'm just filling in a few details. He does the overall design.'

'Would you be able to do something for me, do you think?'

'What do you teach?'

'Music. I'm here part time.' From across the room there is the sound of the photocopier shuddering into life, accompanied by a ragged cheer from the surviving members of the queue.

This would normally have been the signal for Mr Bailey to collect up his papers and wait his turn. It was after all time for the next edition of the cross-cultural 'little magazine' that he published once a month or so. This time however, he just sat looking dazed.

'Cheers.'

Mr Bailey looked up to see the Librarian lifting her glass in his direction. It took him a moment or two to react.

He got up and walked over to her office and, leaning on his elbows, poked his head through the gap in the glass over her desk.

'What is it you are celebrating, if I may ask?'

'Oh, I don't know.' Mrs Booklet thought for a moment. 'Spring?'

As she spoke, she began rummaging through her desk drawer for some kind of container. Finding nothing she looked around on her desk and saw the old yoghurt pot in which she kept paper clips. These she emptied onto the desktop and poured out a very large measure of gin, topping it up with the remains of a bottle of Highland Spring water. As a finishing touch she plucked a bloom from one of the many potted plants that encroached on her workspace and floated it on the surface. She then handed the drink to Mr Bailey. He looked utterly dumbfounded.

'This is most unprofessional. I am afraid that I cannot accept, although I appreciate the kindness of the intention.'

Mr Bailey handed the yoghurt pot gently back through the gap in the glass. The Librarian barred the way with a flail of hands.

'Gooooooorne! Just this once. For Leonard and Virginia.'

Still protesting, but with decreasing vehemence Mr Bailey took firm hold on the carton.

'Bottoms up!'

He gulped down the drink in one, choking only slightly on the fragment of potted plant. The Librarian clapped her hands in delight.

'Better now?'

'Considerably. Was there perhaps some alcohol mixed in? I could hardly taste the spring water.'

'You knew there was, surely.'

'It is only now becoming apparent.'

'What was all that you were saying about being most unprofessional?'

'I meant the imbibing of refreshments outside specified times of the school day. The morning break and the lunch hour.'

'I should have a little lie down if I were you. Otherwise you may find yourself more refreshed than you bargained for. Here

187

take these. They're the keys to my stock cupboard. No one will disturb you in there.'

'I am indebted to you, Mrs. Booklet.'

'Chin chin.'

***

Debbie was about to put the last piece of a particularly fragile kind of Letraset in place on the cover. She had managed to rub it clear of its carrying sheet so that the entire letter was frosted over and ready for the separation phase. She had lifted the bottom half of the sheet away and was debating whether a short sharp tug stood a better chance of effecting a clean break than a slow steady pull.

The gigantic crash against the door of the Resources room resolved matters for her. She jumped and made a very clean break; between the top half of the letter, which was still sticking to the carrier and the bottom half, which was sticking to the artwork.

She had hardly turned round when the door was thrown open to reveal two small girls pulling an enormous trolley. On it were perched the remains of a PA system and behind it stood a tall man, wearing sideburns, flared denim trousers and tinted glasses. These last concealed the complete truth of his feelings on the situation he found himself in, but the straight line of his lips indicated that he was not at all happy. He was Rick, one of the peripatetic instrument teachers, and had been designated wagon master by the head of the Music department. In this capacity he was attempting to keep as much of the equipment as possible from falling from the trolley as it scraped through the door.

At the sound of the crash the door of the inner sanctum opened and Mr. Frack, the MRO, poked his head out. Immediately he saw the cause of the disturbance he turned and went back inside, turning the lock. This only served to make

188

the wagon master look even more unhappy. He underlined this impression by rushing over to the door and, after wrenching the handle a couple of times, starting to hammer on it with his fist.

'Hey, man. How about some help with this gear. None of it's working and we've got a gig tomorrow. Parents' evening.'

There was silence from within, except for the swishing whirr of the electronic stencil cutter. Debbie watched fascinated as the expression on Rick's face mixed from disgruntled to homicidal.

'He said he was going to be rather busy this morning,' she said, as she searched the carrier sheet for a letter to replace the one destroyed in the excitement of the arrival of the stagecoach.

'Really?'

'Cutting stencils for the Music mocks, I think he said.'

Rick's expression softened slightly to a kind of apoplectic sneer.

'You'd better be right.'

He rattled the door handle once more and then walked off past the laden trolley.

'I'll leave the stuff here. Tell him I'll be back to see him after lunch.'

AT SIX THIRTY-SEVEN, PRECISELY...

London, Spring

At six thirty-seven precisely Ralph Furl's key turned in the lock. The exact timing of his arrival home made an airtight fit with the unvaried precision of the post sortie debriefing.

'Evening, Mum. Evening, Dad.'

'Evening, son.'

(He supposed he couldn't really expect his parents to stand to attention).

'Nice cup of tea?'

(He would have to speak to his mother about that cardigan at the next kit inspection).

'Thanks, Mum. I'll just go and wash my hands first.'

(Cue for one of Dad's jokes. Which one of the three would it be tonight?)

'Don't tell me you've dirtied your hands today. I don't know what the Inland Revenue's coming to. Never like that in my day. They'll be putting pit head baths in next.'

(A new one. Ralph couldn't believe it. Something was definitely up.)

'Oh, Jack, leave the boy alone.'

'I'll be down in a jiffy, Mum.'

(That phrase at least was part of the wallpaper.)

Ralph, debriefing over, left the room feeling a little calmer.

Mr Furl cleared his throat.

'Eileen, we're going to have to tell him soon.'

'When the time is right, dear. I know it's very good news for you and me, but it's going to come as a great shock to Ralph. He's a very sensitive boy.'

Mrs Furl resumed laying the table as Ralph returned.

'Are you in tonight, dear?'

190

'Yes, Mum. As I told you, Derek is coming over later to help me analyse the flanking strategies employed at Balaclava.'

'You've lost me already, dear. Supper's at eight. Will Derek be eating with us?'

'Oh, no. Glenda won't let him out of the house without some of her gourmet cooking down his shirt front.'

'There's no need to take it out on her because she doesn't want to mess around with toy soldiers all evening like you two.'

'Mother, for the hundredth time, they are not toys, they are simply aids to our historical research into military strategy.'

'I warned her when Derek started going out with her. 'You'll be a camp follower,' I said.'

'OK, mother. Whatever you say. I think she's pretty well resigned to it by now. Especially as Derek's promised her a ceramic hob when the Crimean War's over.'

Mr Furl cleared his throat again.

'Hmmm! Your mother and I should be so lucky.'

'Let's not start all that again, Jack. Ralph, go up to your room and I'll call you when supper's ready. Jack, I'll come and give you a hand with that shelf in a moment.

***

The soldiers stood in perfect formation, staring into space, their uniforms authentic to the last frog and epaulette. One or two casualties from the previous skirmish still lay where they had fallen, awaiting medical attention.

Ralph finished his cup of tea and threw the dice. A six. Hard choice. More rations or more ammunition. Only one mule train was allowed through. The Russian position looked vulnerable, but given the severity of the winter (he knew for a fact that there had been heavy falls of snow along that front) ...

'Boredom, boredom
ba-dum, ba-dum!'

That rather plain boy next door seemed to have acquired a record player for his birthday. Ralph looked across the narrow passageway dividing his house from the next. In the opposite bedroom he could see Master Ordinary doing the most extraordinary things in front of the mirror. He was jumping up and down in approximate time with the beat, twisting and shaking his head from side to side like an epileptic sperm.

As he did so his schoolboy fringe was swirling around, bits of it beginning to stick to his forehead. The crowning touch, which made Ralph smile despite himself, was the fact that he was wearing a pair of dark glasses exactly like the ones that that Ralph remembered his own mother wearing when he was a kid.

It was obvious that there was no one else in the house, otherwise one of Tom's parents would surely have put a stop to this by now. He'd go through the bedroom floor if he went on like that much longer. Perhaps that was the idea.

Ralph's own mother and father had never neglected him like that. They were never out when he came home. Never went anywhere without giving advance notice. Three weeks minimum. That way, you knew where you were. Always the same. Mr and Mrs Furl downstairs, son and heir upstairs … It would be a shock for them, when he told them. A shock for everyone.

Ralph pulled the window shut and drew the curtains. The music sounded almost as loud as ever. He turned back towards the tabletop battlefield.

'I've got to tell them, Derek. And you've got to tell Glenda.'

'Don't you know there's a war on?'

'I'm serious.'

'I know, love. Let's just finish this part of the campaign at least. Then we can decide how to break it to them.'

'You promise?'

'I promise. … It's still your move I think.'

'I know. I can't decide between food or munitions. You look so well dug in over there I don't know whether to starve you or blast you.'

Derek walked round the table, put his arms round Ralph.

'Ooh! You're such a tease,' he said, and tried to kiss him.

Ralph froze for a moment, and then squirmed free.

'Derek, for God's sake! Not here! Mum'll be up with a cup of tea any minute.'

Derek looked at his watch in rather a laboured fashion.

'Any minute? You mean eight fifty-four precisely, don't you?'

Ralph ignored him and walked over to the window. Bracing himself, he opened it and pulled back the curtains.

'Anarchy for the UK,

it's coming sometime and maybe… '

The music was, if possible, even more deafening. Tom was still jumping about but at the same time scooping gobbets of white goo onto his hair from a glass jar. He then made towelling-dry movements with his hands until his head looked like a porcupine in shock.

Derek was very amused.

'You never said you lived next door to a punk rocker.'

'We didn't. He was just another snotty little swot up till now. Quiet as a mouse.'

'Never again I'm afraid. He'll be all safety pins and bin liners by next week. Then you'll really have something to moan about.' As he was speaking, Derek walked over to where Ralph was standing, and began gently massaging his shoulders.

Ralph was by now so mesmerised by Tom's behaviour and the overpowering beat that appeared to be the sole cause of it that he put up only token resistance this time.

'I've told you. Not here.' He murmured as he made a half-hearted attempt to free himself, and then let himself relax under the firm pressure of Derek's fingers.

'Whatever you say, love.' said Derek, and dug in a little deeper. 'Mustn't upset the tea lady. Mind you, I'll bet you she knows already. Mine does, although I'm sure she'll make every effort to appear flabbergasted when our little secret gets out. So as not to disappoint us. My father will merely revolve in his grave a couple of times.'

There was a knock on the door. The two men scrambled to their positions either side of the table. As Ralph did so, he swept a few of his infantrymen onto the floor with his elbow. Going down on his knees to pick them up, he shouted,

'Come in.'

'Nice cup of tea for you both?' Mrs Furl always made a question of it.

Derek checked his watch again and made a circle of his thumb and forefinger as he smiled at Ralph.

'Oh, thanks, Mum.'

Mrs Furl came in and winced.

'What an awful racket. I'll have to get your father to go round and ask his parents to tell him to turn it down.'

'The Watsons are out for the evening, Mum.'

'And he'd never hear the doorbell, I'm afraid, Mrs Furl.'

Mrs Furl put down the mugs of tea and strode to the window. Leaning out as far as she could she shouted,

'Tom, please would you turn the noise down.'

Tom continued his jumping up and down, and as if to spite her bounced over to the record player and turned up the volume even higher.

'TURN ... IT ... DOWN !'

'He's totally oblivious, Mrs Furl.'

'Oh, is he?' Mrs Furl turned from the window to where Ralph was squatting mopping up the last of the troops. 'Give me some of those, will you, Ralph.'

'The twenty-fifth Hussars?'

'Yes, they'll do. And one of those things on wheels.'

'The forty mil howitzer?'

'Fine.'

'Anything else you'd like?'

'No, this lot should do the trick.' Mrs Furl worked her hands together as if she was moulding a snowball, then spun on her heel and flung her fistful of lead hard at Tom's open bedroom window.

Fortunately for Tom he was bending down over his record player ready to put on the Buzzcocks yet again, and so the volley sailed harmlessly over the small of his back and crashed against the wall. Alerted by the scatter of unfamiliar playthings about his feet he looked up, just in time to see Mrs Furl slam the window shut and draw the curtains.

***

The next morning, Saturday, Tom was having breakfast with his parents, Mike and Patricia Watson.

Having been unable to get the Brylcreem out of his hair, Tom had it very neatly combed, a fact that puzzled Patricia considerably as she had never seen her son as a bank clerk. Mike, who was nursing the down side of a brief but intense encounter with the European wine lake the previous evening, emerged from behind the Daily Express only when necessary, strictly for reasons of survival rather than sociability.

Patricia couldn't understand the rules for this week's Guardian Prize Crossword let alone solve any of the clues, and, having drawn the chauffeur's straw last night, felt at a clear headed although slightly irritable loose end.

She had recently completed the research for a programme about sex stereotyping in children's toys and was therefore intrigued to see that Tom, who had always been given a choice (underlined) and had at different times nursed dolls and kitted out action men, seemed to be showing signs of exactly that post

195

pubescent hard core militarism that she had been hearing about from other members of her group.

His bowl of cereal was flanked by two rather squashed looking tin soldiers of the type her two older brothers had spent hours playing with when she was a little girl.

'I haven't seen those before, darling. Where did you get them from?'

'Next door.'

'From Ralph?'

'No. Mrs Furl. She threw them at me. Through my bedroom window.'

'Threw them at you. How bizarre. Did they hurt you?'

'No, they all missed me.'

'All? How many?'

'Six, plus a howitzer.'

'Howitzer?'

The Daily Express trembled and spoke.

'It's a kind of cannon, darling.'

'Oh, you are awake, Mike. Did you hear that? She threw six soldiers and a howitzer at Tom.'

The Express mumbled something suitable to the occasion.

Pat threw down her napkin and rose from the table. 'I'm going round to speak to that woman right away.'

'M-u-u-m!' Tom feared nothing more than the prospect of his mother creating an embarrassing scene.

Not having the strength left to groan, Mike pulled down the newsprint barricade and spoke in a soft would-be persuasive monotone.

'Darling, perhaps we should hear the full story. A bit of research? You're so good at that sort of thing, darling.'

'If you promise me you won't go into hiding again.'

Mike inclined his head just enough to indicate gracious acquiescence without causing the red-hot ball bearings to collide in his forehead again.

'Right. Question one. Why was Mrs Hurl furling … er … Furl hurling - tin soldiers at you till all hours last night? And question two, why are you looking like Mr Brass the Bank Manager this morning?

***

Mrs Furl was standing in the same place as she had been the night before, looking across at Tom's bedroom.
'I really am sorry, Ralph. I don't know what came over me. I've never done anything like that before. Never. Derek was ever so nice about it, although it must have meant a wasted journey for him. Don't suppose you got much of a game with half your toy soldiers missing … I just felt so cross I could have strangled the boy.'
Ralph looked up from his regimental dispatches. To cover his mother's action he had written. 'Just prior to nightfall there was an act of God in the form of a bolt of lightning which instantly killed five of our men and melted a howitzer beyond recognition.' It made a change from all that dice throwing.
 'Don't worry, mother. We managed to scrub round it and he beat me in the end, so he was very chuffed.'
Mrs Furl brightened.
'That's nice, dear.'
'Yes, I should have seen it a mile off. I was down to my last string of mules and reinforcements were a day and a half's march away. Not to mention that nasty outbreak of cholera a day or so back. How could he fail?'
'I'm sure I don't know, dear.'
 Ralph put down his pen, with the historically correct steel nib, in the trough of the period writing slope that he had managed to unearth in a local antique market, and leaned comfortably back in his seat.
'Y-e-e-s. I think it was a case of learning the wrong lesson from history. I was trying to be less foolhardy than Raglan and

197

co were originally and this made me overcautious. I couldn't think on my feet at all.'

'Never mind, dear … Do you think I ought to go and apologise? It would be neighbourly.'

'Much more neighbourly than his behaviour.'

Just at that moment there was a tap on the door and Mr Furl came in.

'There's someone to see you both.' he said, and ushered in Tom and his mother. He cleared his throat. 'It's Mrs Watson and her son.'

'Yes, Jack, I can see that. What can I do for you?'

'First of all, I'd like to know whether you threw these at my son last night.' Patricia was holding out a palm full of the casualties mentioned in dispatches towards Mrs Furl. As she did so Mr Furl suddenly remembered that the kettle needed attending to in some pressingly urgent fashion. Tom showed signs of wanting to go and help him.

'Stay here, Tom, I want to get to the bottom of this once and for all.'

Mrs Furl was about to reply when Ralph said,

'Those men were under my command, and I therefore take full responsibility.'

Patricia let slip a couple of daggers in Tom's direction.

'May I ask what provoked you, exactly?'

'He kept playing one of his records over and over again very loudly and I just got fed up. I shouted at him a couple of times but he didn't hear.'

'Is this true, Tom.'

'No. I was playing two records, not one, and they were only on maximum for a little while.'

'But you're positive that Mrs Furl threw these at you.'

'I didn't actually see her do it. I just suddenly saw them on the carpet, and when I looked up Mrs Furl was closing Ralph's bedroom window.'

Patricia drew a deep breath and said brightly,
'Perhaps we should settle for apologies all round, then.'

ANCIENT GREEK

London, Spring

The following Monday the Frognal College playground at mid-morning break was as ever an inventory of the human behaviour permissible in public under current legislation; from struggling heaps of first year boys to sixth formers patrolling the rose walk hoping not to have to report their classmates for smoking behind the fives courts.

Tom, a first year, felt doubly new. Most of the rest of his class had been together in the Junior Branch, and those that had not had been here for six months. He had, until last week been at a fairly tough mixed comprehensive. This difference in background would normally have made him the target for a certain amount of peer group pressure to conform but as he was quite big nobody dared make the first move. The puppyish tumblings of his classmates held no terrors for him after rather more serious encounters elsewhere.

He had just taken out his diary to check the matrix number on the Buzzcocks record when from the heap of blazers arms and legs that was tumbling slowly in his direction he heard the sound of real pain and tears.

Tom got up and ran over and then dived into the scrum and pulled out a short dark haired boy. Having scattered the tormentors, he offered the victim a Polo mint.

'Thanks.' Sniff.

'Do they often do that to you?'

'Only about once a week these days.' Filthy handkerchief dabbed in right eye. 'It usually happens after double Ancient Greek. It seems to upset them, and then they take it out on me.'

'How long have they been doing it?'

'About six months. Ever since I came here really.'

'That's terrible. Why don't you tell someone? What's your name, by the way?'

'Ian. I did once. We all got kept in after school and they beat the shit out of me for a whole week.'

'What about your parents?'

'Mum was horrified. But my father just laughs. He says it was far worse for him when he was here. The way he talks he seems almost proud of it. He's always talking about the 'old days' as if they were some distant golden age. It was only fifteen years ago.'

Ian blew his nose and with a final wipe round from chin to forehead put his handkerchief back in his trouser pocket.

'So he thinks being bullied is just carrying on the family tradition?'

'Yes, in a way.' Ian sniffed loudly but it had a more cheerful sound to it, like a kind of inhaled laugh.

'You're going to have to learn to stand up for yourself.'

'That's easy for you to say. You're bigger than me.'

'At least you can tell me next time it looks like happening.'

'It looks like happening every Monday morning for the rest of the year. After double Ancient Greek.'

***

That evening at supper the Marten family listened in silence for a whole minute as Ian told them what had happened that morning.

The twins, Ben and Jacob, contented themselves with heated but, for a change, whispered recounts of each other's allocation of baked beans.

Sophie, an art school Siouxsie Sioux look alike, was there to prove to her mother, Sarah, that she didn't treat the place like a hotel. Despite herself she found her little brother's adventures quite interesting for once.

'And he had to rescue you? Ah, diddums.'

Ian rose reliably to the bait. It was something she really missed at college.

'How would you like it?' he shouted indignantly.

'Twelve blokes on top of me?' Sophie paused for the full Mae West effect, as seen on TV recently. 'Well … '

Sarah didn't like getting 'heavy' with any of her children, but …

'That's enough, Sophie. Eat up your broccoli. It'll make your hair curl.'

'I don't want it to curl, Sarah. I want it like it is. Nice and spiky.' She preened herself, pulling a few ends into suitable disarray. The twins looked up aghast from their bean counting.

'It looks horrible … sixty-eight, sixty-nine, seventy.'

'You got two more than me.'

'Shut your face, you two.'

Much though he hated the 'patriarchal trip,' to the extent that his department was a legend in local government for inefficiency because he never delegated anything, Chris felt it was time to participate. Yes, to intervene even. He would just have to accept the bad karma that this might entail.

'Look, mate. If this is really getting to be a hassle, I'll go and have a word with Old Salami for you if you like.'

'No, it's all right, Chris. Like you said, it never did you any harm. I expect it's character forming.'

Chris tried not to make his sigh of relief too audible.

'OK, mate. You just have to say.'

'Sure.'

Sarah had fewer qualms about the karmic consequences of intervention.

'Darling, I can't make out if you're being totally serious. They're not really all jumping on you at once … still? I thought Chris was exaggerating when he used to tell me about it.'

'Yes, still. It's become a school tradition, like the Eton Wall Game or something.'

Although she couldn't stop herself laughing at her son's mournful expression, Sarah remained uneasy.

'Chris, I really do think we ought to go and see the Headmaster about this. This isn't pre-war Germany you know.'

'Pre-war Germany? You can't be serious. A little playground rough and tumble … '

'Twelve to one? I call that regimented bullying.'

'It won't be so bad now I've got someone on my side.'

'Your knight in shining plimsolls. What's his name, anyway.'

'Watson.'

'Why don't you invite 'Watson' round for tea after school one day next week,' Sarah suggested. 'I'd like to meet him. He sounds very nice.'

'He is.' Ian shot a glance at Sophie. 'Even if he does like punk rock.'

There is a chorus of disgust from all except Sophie.

'Sounds like a really good bloke.'

Sarah leant across and patted her on the arm.

'Oooh! Watch out! You'll make someone jealous talking like that. Besides, he's a little young for you, I would have thought.'

'All I said was, he sounds like a good bloke. Anyway, 'Someone' can stuff it for all I care.'

Chris raised his eyes to the ceiling.

'Not another row, surely?'

'Just musical differences. I mean, Elton John.' Sophie all but spat on the carpet.

'Is he still going? We used to like him.'

He began to sing, with great gusto and minimal accuracy of pitch,

'Fly away, you skyline pigeon, fly… '

Ian and the bean counters screamed in unison and scattered from the table. Sophie stalked after them out of the room, leaving Chris and Sarah alone.

As the door slammed Chris stopped singing instantly and gave a beaming smile.

'Old Golden Tonsils strikes again. I never could stand the blighter personally.'

'No, you were more of a closet Jethro Tull man, as I recall.'

'Closet? I was quite prepared to play the flute standing on one leg anywhere, any time, absolutely without shame. I still am, come to that.'

'Promise me it won't come to that. Promise me.'

TWIRP

London, Spring

It was the school dance at Frognal College. 'Hooray Henry's Disco' was pumping out the music. It was largely progressive rock, Genesis, Yes, Deep Purple, with a smattering of the top twenty. Tom was hanging around at the edge of things, hoping to be asked to lend a hand and flipping through the singles box while the DJ wasn't looking. The only remotely punkish thing available was Eddie and the Hotrods. Tom had marked it down as a near miss. Right speed but without the attitude. As he shrank back into the shadows, Sophie walked up with Semi-ex in tow.

She stood directly in front of the DJ and shouted,
'Got any Sex Pistols?'
'For this lot? You must be joking.'
'No punk at all?'
'None at all. Sorry.'
Tom reached inside his donkey jacket and walked forward a few paces.
'I've got the Buzzcocks.'
The DJ looked at him with contemptuous incredulity.
'What did you say?'
Sophie said slowly,
'Buzz … cocks.'
'Spiral Scratch,' Tom chimed in with great fervour.
'Really?' The DJ all but patted Tom on the head.
'It's the name of the record,' said Sophie coldly. She snatched it from Tom and thrust it at the DJ.
'Are you going to play it, or what?'
'Since you ask so politely, I'll think about it.'
'What is there to think about?'

'Ooh, let's see. Audience reaction … lynch mobs … might even get sent to see the Headmaster. You never know.'

'Well, if you're too chicken, he'll do it,' said Sophie pointing at Tom.

'Who, me?'

'It's your record.'

Tom glanced at the DJ, who shrugged.

'Be my guest.'

'But I'm not sure how it all works. Properly.'

'You must do. You've been watching me all evening.'

Sophie urged Tom towards the record deck with a sweep of her hand.

'Garn. Avvago.'

The record ended and the DJ sat back with an 'it's all yours' gesture. Tom gulped and then went to work. After a bit of fumbling and some quite impressive feedback screech from the microphone, he managed to get the record playing.

With a brief nod of thanks Sophie started a wild pogo. Tom felt honour bound to do likewise, then found he could not stop. As the spotlight picked them out the other dancers turned to watch.

About half way though the record Sophie's semi-detached boyfriend walked over to the DJ and began whispering in his ear. The DJ reached across and the music cut dead. There was a short pause and then the next record came on, David Bowie's 'Rebel, Rebel.'

After a few defiant salmon leaps Sophie stopped and went over to speak to her Semi-ex.

'What the fuck did you do that for?'

Tom had meanwhile put his record back in its sleeve and under his donkey jacket.

'To stop you making a fool of yourself with that little twirp. He's a first former, for God's sake. He's not even supposed to be here.'

'You're the twirp. Who do you think you are? I'll dance with who I like and how I like.'

'Not while you're going out with me, you don't. I'll be a laughing stock in the Sixth Form Common Room tomorrow.'

'In that case you'll just have to find someone less twirpish to go out with, won't you? More suited to your wisdom and maturity … not to mention your Oxbridge Entrance.'

Semi-ex had turned pale.

'If that's what you want. Anyway, I don't think I'm going to make it to Oxford, the way you've been messing me around. Dressing up all weird. Acting like a teenager.'

'Which I am. And so are you.'

'You know what I mean. You just don't act your age any more.'

'You mean I don't act your age any more. Why should I?'

'No reason … You really worry me, you know. Chopping and changing. I mean, this punk thing. You don't really like it, do you? It's never going to last.'

'What's it to you?'

'There you go. More aggression. Straight out of the Punk Mail Order Catalogue.'

'Why do you see everything I do as a deviation from your norm? Why not try and see it my way for a change. I'm not breaking your rules, just sticking to mine. I mean, even your boring old fart, Daddy Dylan, said 'to live outside the law, you must be honest.' I'm just trying to be honest, if that's OK with you.'

'Fine, go ahead.' As Semi-ex turned on his heel he said, 'Just let me know when Johnny Rotten comes up with a song fit for Dylan to wipe his arse on.'

Sophie looked hurt and almost burst into tears. Then she composed herself and walked back to Tom, who was still hovering awkwardly near the disco.

'Looks like we're not wanted round here, mate. Do you mind walking to the station with me? … What's your name, by the way?'

'Tom.'

'Not very punk, is it?'

'No, not really.'

'How about Tommy?'

'A bit better, I suppose.'

'What's your sir name?'

'Not at all punk.'

'Oh… Let's see… I know. In the first world war the British soldiers turned German insults into compliments by calling themselves The Old Contemptibles.'

'Tommy Contemptible, you mean.'

'No, you prat. Think of any insults you've had lately.'

Tom thought for a moment.

'Well, Johnson did call me a twirp. But all the sixth formers call the first years that.'

'Brilliant!' Sophie clapped her hands together and laughed. 'OK, Tommy Twirp, let's go.' Sophie clutched Tom's arm and led him from the hall, Buzzcocks in hand.

***

New York, Spring

Margaret was in a meeting with her head of department. She leaned towards him across the table to emphasise the strength of her argument.

' … only this time, it's Spitting London, not Swinging London. I really think the time is right for a Special Update on the whole city, Dan.' Margaret reminded herself not to oversell the project. As Head of Special Projects, Dan Gitler liked to have his own ideas.

'You really think this Punk Rock thing is that important. Rolling Stone doesn't rate it at all.'

'Forget Rolling Stone, Dan. They have no idea. How could they. They don't have their ear to the ground in every dismal outer suburb of London and Manchester.'

'But you do.' Dan smiled that patronising smile. The one that said, 'I can call you nigger with no hang ups 'cos I'm an old hippie, so that's cool, man.' It always made Margaret want to gag.

'Through my contacts, yes.'

'And what do they say? These 'contacts'?' Dan looked at his watch just unsubtly enough for Margaret to notice.

She leaned forward again and pushed a couple of audio cassettes and some xeroxed magazines to his side of the desk. Dan craned his neck round to read what was written on them.

' 'Sniffin' Glue'? John Peel? You gotta be kidding!' He leafed through the magazines and glanced at the cassettes. Then he looked up at Margaret. 'You seriously think it's worth a special. An hour long special about what a bunch of bored little Brits get up to? The British press say they're all Nazis anyway. You wouldn't want to do something about the Klan instead, maybe?'

Another patronising smile. He'd be giving her the not quite latest soul brother handshake any time now.

'I think that's maybe more your line of country,' Margaret tried to make it sound like the ultimate compliment. As she watched Dan's smile go into spasm, she said. 'How about I go over there and have a look round, come up with a treatment. Give me say … a fortnight?'

Dan went into his 'just between friends' plantation owner act. 'You nigger bitches sure drive a hard bargain.' He rocked with laughter at his own daring. 'We'll say ten days and not a cotton pickin' minute more, y'all understand?'

Margaret said nothing except to raise her right arm and clench her fist. She was not smiling.

***

London, Spring

It was the philosophy of Frognal College to keep alive the spirit of Renaissance Boy for as long as possible, at least until the shadow of the GCE lengthened to such an extent that the 'serious' subjects -English, Maths and Ancient Greek, blotted out the frivolities of Music and Art.

Hence the sound of seventeen recorders attempting to reach agreement on the tune of 'Au Clair de la Lune'. Tom had just managed to stifle a fit of the giggles by staring resolutely at the ceiling and was launching into the next bar with everything under control, when he noticed that the music teacher was staring directly at him. So were sixteen other pairs of eyes.

'OK, Watson. Cool it, man.' The music teacher, known behind his back as Rockstar, smiled at Tom. 'Let's get the tune right before we try the flashy solos.' He walked over to where Tom was standing, and arranged his fingers over the correct holes. 'Now, blow.' As Tom did so, the teacher moved his fingers for him until a close approximation of the tune was completed. There was ragged applause from the rest of the class, with one or two cries of 'encore'.

Rockstar smiled grimly.

'Let's not push our luck.'

A voice from down the row asked innocently,

'Did you ever play recorder, sir, when you were in that rock band?'

This brought forth a chorus of derision,

'Don't be stupid. Sir played drums / lead guitar / xylophone / bass / triangle …' The supposed choice of instrument became increasingly far fetched, until finally 'Sir' was forced to laugh, and with a thankful glance at the clock ceased for a moment to be an accessory after the fact in the murder of the muse. He waved them to silence.

'OK, you know the scene. If anyone comes in, you're carrying out running repairs and maintenance on your instruments.'

As he spoke the class began to unscrew their recorders and to give them a desultory polish with odd bits of Kleenex.

'As you very well know,' he went on, 'I played rhythm guitar.'

'Like Keith Richards, sir?'

'Yeah,' 'Sir' said with a perfectly straight face, 'he copped a few licks off me.'

The class smiled in unison at this obvious fantasy and settled down for their weekly dose of the rock'n'roll fairy tale.

**

It was Saturday night Sophie and her Semi-Ex were hanging round the telephone kiosks at Golders Green bus station waiting for news of a party.

She was reaching the end of the numbers in her address book and would shortly have to start cadging off complete strangers. This was almost always bad news; parents upstairs, no spirits, or, once, soft drinks only, and nine times out of ten, lousy music - parents' records and/or the current top twenty.

Semi-ex looked round to trawl for familiar faces. He recognised that kid in first year, waiting for the 210. He nudged Sophie.

'Why not ask your new boyfriend?' Sophie followed his gaze.

'Him? He just walked me to the tube, that's all.' She turned back and tried one of the early, unanswered numbers again. A parent replied. Sophie put down the phone without speaking. She looked back to where Tom was standing.

'Might as well ask, I suppose.'

She walked over to him.

'Hello, Twirp. Where you off to then?'

211

'Oh, hi. Just round to a friend's house.'

'Party?'

'No. We've been writing some songs together and we're making a demo tape this evening to send round to a few record companies.'

'What sort of songs?'

Tom looked closely at the bus timetable set in the concrete pillar.

'The usual. You know. Fast and angry.' He stole a glance at her reaction.

Sophie looked round for Semi-ex. He had disappeared.

'Sounds good. I'd like to hear them.'

Tom turned bright red.

'What, now do you mean?'

'No, you berk, not standing at this sodding bus stop.'

'Oh, I see.'

Tom craned his neck to see if any bus was about to arrive. It wasn't.

'So where does he live? Your friend.'

'Finchley.'

To Sophie the word Finchley had the same perversely intriguing ring to it as Bromley, home of the notorious Contingent, who had been in at the start of things and with whom her idol Siouxsie had been closely associated. Maybe there was something there for her.

She looked round. Still no sign of Semi-ex. He must have pissed off.

'Any chance of me coming with you? Having a listen?'

Tom turned pale. He had a vision of Johnson and all his friends crowding round him blind side of the fives courts, followed by many different kinds of physical assault.

'Won't Johnson mind?'

'Who the hell's Johnson?' Then Sophie remembered. 'Oh, him. It's none of his business.'

'He's still going to beat me up.'

'Did he last time?'

'No,' Tom was forced to admit. 'but he did give me some very nasty looks.'

'That's as far as it will go this time, I promise. Or he'll get no for an answer.'

'How do you mean?'

'Never you mind.' Sophie shivered. 'So, you gonna phone your mate, or what?'

D. I. Y.

London, Spring

The first problem was, how far away from the mike to put the
Rolf Harris Stylophone so that it didn't drown out the voices,
and then how far away to put the cardboard box so that when
Jake hit it with the serving spoons it didn't drown them all out.
 Most of the other problems had to do with Mrs Wilson putting
her head round the door, either to offer cups of tea or ask them
to be a little quieter because of Mr Wilson's migraine. After
several attempts they had hit on an acceptably raw version of
'Reject Romance' and now sat round exhausted.
 Jake turned to Sophie.
 'What do you think?'
 She thought for a moment.
 'It's not the Clash, but it's got something. Definitely.' The two
boys exchanged cautious, pleased smiles. 'The only thing is, I
don't think any record company is going to go for it. Not as it
stands.'
 Tom and Jake began to look unhappy.
 'So, what do you suggest we do?'
 'DIY. Start our own label. Peel's sure to play it.'
 'Do you think so?' Tom was doubtful.
 'Bound to.'
 'But how's he going to play it if there's no 'it' to play?' Jake
asked. 'If we start our own label, that means we've got to know
how to make a record, and we don't.'
 'We could ask, I suppose,' said Tom.' There's that shop just by
Camden Town tube that sells all that rock'n'roll and punk. They
might know where records come from.'
 Sophie laughed,
 'They'll probably say that a great big stork leaves them in the
doorway once a week. Worth a try though.'

Jake was still unconvinced.

'Of course the other problem is we haven't got a proper group yet. It's just us two. We need a couple more people, somewhere to rehearse, money to buy instruments with … '

'Stuff rehearsals. Stuff buying instruments,' Sophie said. 'All we need is people. Maybe bass and rhythm guitar, that's all. There's loads of people around with that sort of gear. I can probably get Johnson to lend me his bass next time he stops posing in front of his mirror with it.'

'And we could ask Rockstar to come along,' Tom said to Jake.' He might agree, just for laughs.'

'Who's he?' Sophie asked.

'Just a bloke who teaches music at our school.'

Sophie threw her head back in disgust.

'Fu-u-u-uckin' 'ell! A teacher? He'll be far too old.'

'Beggars can't be choosers,' said Tom with a sort of owlish wisdom that made Sophie smile to herself.

'No, maybe you're right. Tell you what. We'll get him in for the recording, then ditch him for someone who looks right when we start playing live. That's what the Pistols did, after all.'

Tom looked doubtful.

'I don't think that would be fair, really.'

'Fair?' Sophie exclaimed. 'Fair? We can't have an old hippie cluttering up the stage. We'll never get anywhere like that.'

Jake, who had said nothing for quite a while suddenly said,

'I think, as it's our songs it should be our decisions. I mean, we should decide who's in the band or whatever.'

'Fine. I was only trying to help. Do it your own way.'

Sophie slumped back in her chair, affecting indifference.

Tom said,

'Maybe be we could just have a go at recording something, and then if it works out we could form a proper band afterwards. Depending on whether people bought the record.'

Jake was unconvinced.

'We still don't know how to.'

'Better ask teacher,' Sophie said sweetly.

***

A few days later, Rockstar, known to his friends as Rick and to the Inland Revenue Special Investigations Section as Mr Temple - open brackets, cross check with other aliases, close brackets - was sitting on the lower deck of the 38 bus at Dalston Junction waiting for the usual scrummage of passengers trying to get on and off to subside. He was on his way home to his basement flat after another day in the life of a peripatetic music teacher. Frognal College was the last on his weekly round and was his favourite not only because it paid better than his official ILEA work but because he'd managed to wangle it under the heading of freelance work and it wasn't taxed at source. Besides, the kids there were frighteningly well behaved compared to some of the other dumps he taught in.

Take today for instance. Not only did they all play in tune for several bars in a row, but two of them actually came up to him afterwards to ask his advice.

'Sir, we want to know how to make a record.' Rick realised that he didn't have a clue. He'd been in any number of recording studios of course, but after the master mix left the control room? No idea. That was all down to the producers.

He glanced over his shoulder to check it was still there and then fought his way off the bus and walked up to the musical instrument shop.

It was a long time since he'd bought his last wah-wah pedal there but he seemed to remember the guy saying something about a four-track in the basement.

***

'So you reckon you've discovered the new Lennon and
McCartney and you fancy yourself as their player manager.
Quite a team; couple of Twirps, a teacher and you on bass.'
 Semi-ex, having yet again failed to get Sophie's knickers off,
was consoling himself with a particularly intricate though silent
bass run, with a few pouting glances in his bedroom mirror for
good measure.
'Something like that. Only I won't be their manager. They're
pretty sussed. I'll just play.'
'My bass.'
'Yeah.'
Another supple, subtle run.
'Tell you what. Why don't you sing, and I'll play bass?'
Sophie was speechless for a moment.
'I don't believe it. Spend all you life slagging me off for being
a punk, and now you wanna be in my gang.'
 'I didn't say I wanted to be in the group, I just thought you'd
like a little help. But if you prefer to make total musical prats
of yourselves, it's up to you.' Semi-ex plucked a few more
silently exquisite notes from his instrument.
 'Very thoughtful of you. However they haven't asked me to
sing. Tom's going to.'
'Tom?'
 'My new boyfriend, as you insist on calling him.'
There was the sound of string snapping sharply and
unmusically against fret.
'Watson? That little jerk? He'll be useless.'
'I don't think so.'
 Semi-ex did not respond directly, but began playing the base
line to Roxy Music's 'Love is the Drug'. He sang the refrain to
Sophie in an exaggeratedly pointed way that made her smile
despite herself.
 'Nice try, Bryan, but wrong,' Sophie said. 'Now, is there any
chance of my being able to do my homework?' Sophie pulled

217

out a grubby piece of paper from her pocket and handed it to Semi-ex. 'They reckon I'll have six notes to deal with.'
 Semi-ex stared at the paper with an expression of mounting disbelief,
 'These are lyrics?'
 'Sure.'
 'And music?'
 'Yep.'
 'And which are your six then?'
 Sophie stood up from the sofa and came across to look over his shoulder.
 'That one, that one, that one, those two and… oh, yeah that one over there.' She stabbed a finger at the bottom left hand corner of the paper.
 'And you're quite sure they told you this was a song?' Semi-ex sounded grave, like a television detective questioning the slightly sub-normal victim of a serious sex offence.
 'No, they just made a racket. But I liked it.'
 Semi-ex shook his head.
 'This I've got to see.' He presented Sophie with his guitar as if it was the centrepiece of a banquet.

***

On a drizzly Friday evening Tom and Jake stood outside the music shop. The window was lit, but there was no sign of life from within, and nobody they recognised on the street.
 Jake turned and looked across at the Club Four Aces and then back at Tom.
 'Do you reckon any one will turn up?'
 'Hope so. Or we'll have to do it ourselves. All of it.'
 'If we can get in.'
 Suddenly, in the distance they saw a familiar figure carrying a guitar case walking towards them. Tom felt a prickle of excitement. Jake, who was looking the other way, noticed a

small car crawling along the kerb. It stopped and he saw Sophie waving to them. She got out and came over.

'Hi.' She noticed the drumsticks sticking out from Jake's breast pocket. 'Thought those were chopsticks for a moment.' She looked back at the car. 'I've brought Johnson with me. Hope you don't mind. He wouldn't lend me his guitar otherwise.'

Jake was about to say something extremely discouraging when Mr Temple arrived.

'Hello, sir,' said Tom.

'Hi.' Rick peered through the shop door.' Engineer not arrived yet? I told him seven thirty.'

The car door slammed and Semi-ex walked over, carrying another guitar case.

He nodded to Tom and Jake and then said,

'Hello, sir. Come to cut another hit record?'

Rick smiled but said nothing.

There was the sound of a bolt being drawn and then the shop door scraped open. Rick recognised the young Greek Cypriot assistant he had negotiated with earlier in the week. The assistant swept his long frizzy hair behind his ears and smiled uncertainly at each of them in turn.

'This your band?' he asked Rick.

Jake said firmly,

'We don't belong to anyone, actually.'

'Fair enough.' The assistant turned and led the way through the shop and down some stairs at the back into a basement room.

After the light had been turned on they were able to discern a drum kit set up in one corner, a battered looking keyboard and a couple of mike stands deep in conversation and two speaker cabinets. One end of the room was partitioned off to form a recording control booth.

' S'all yours,' the Assistant said with a sweep of the hand.

Rick turned to Tom and Jake.

'So how do you want to play this?'

'As fast and loud as possible, sir,' said Jake.

The Assistant, whose name turned out to be Andy, exchanged tired exasperated glances with Semi-ex. Sophie looked very hard at the Marc Bolan poster on the wall.

'Yeah, sure. But what? You know. Words. . . music. Things like that.'

Tom reached into the inside pocket of his anorak and drew out photocopies of the document that had so startled Semi-ex earlier in the week. He handed them out.

Rick studies his for a moment.

'Certainly different,' he said.' I take it 'S' means singer, 'B' means bass, and so on.'

'Yes, sir,' said Tom. 'It seemed easier that way.'

Andy had dragged back his copy into the recording lair and was reading it through while attempting to set some levels.

Semi-ex was sharing a copy with Sophie, in between unpacking and plugging in his guitar. Rick was doing likewise, to-ing and fro-ing with the control room and making small adjustments to the controls on his channel.

He spoke quietly to Andy.

'Whatever happens, make sure there's plenty of phasing on my track. I'm really into that.'

Andy shrugged. Phasing seemed a bit passé to him, but who was he to argue.

Jake was adjusting the height of his drum stool and making some experimental forays on more percussion than he had ever dreamed of banging a serving spoon on.

Tom was reading through his own words, wondering why they suddenly made absolutely no sense to him whatsoever, and singing the odd line when Andy asked him to over the headphones.

Semi-ex whispered to Sophie,

'Don't forget. If he can't cut it, just grab the mike and sing.'

Sophie looked up from the fourth of her six notes.

'I'll think about it.'

Beyond her amp she could see the sound man, or whatever he was called, standing in the doorway of his hutch.

Andy cupped his hands round his mouth and shouted above the din.

'Ready when you are.'

Jake, seeing that Tom hadn't heard, got up from behind his kit and, lifting one of the earphones said,

'He's ready.'

Tom turned round and gave Andy a thumbs-up.

'Do you want to go for a take straight away?' Andy asked.

'You might as well,' Rick said to Tom. 'Tape's cheap.'

'Yes, I think we will.'

Tom suddenly felt totally in control, fearless.

'If you could start the tape,' he said to Andy.' I'll count us in. We can always cut out the beginning later, can't we?'

'Sure.'

Andy went into the control room. There was a tense silence, then Tom heard over the phones, 'Rolling.'

Tom counted up to four.

From the moment Tom started to sing Sophie knew that Semi-ex was out of her life; Jake knew that his music really did fit Tom's words; Rick knew that he would never understand; Semi-ex knew that he was part of the problem, not the solution; and Andy knew that he'd have to mix the phasing very low.

As they sat waiting for the playback there was a silence as each of them thought about how their lives had changed.

Semi-ex made one last effort to solve his own problem by creating another one.

'Pity about the vocals.' He smiled sympathetically at Tom. 'Maybe if Sophie was to have a go. I'd be happy to help out on bass, if you want.'

Sophie was outraged.

'Don't talk such crap. You were great, Tom. And I reckon my playing sounded all right.'

Semi-ex turned for support from a fellow musician.

'How about you, sir. What do you think?'

Rick thought for a moment.

'I don't know what I think. It's not really my scene at all, but I quite liked it.'

The second track was a page from the telephone book reading in a rising scream to drums and rhythm guitar. It took five minutes. They called it 'Phoney'.

WIND UP

London, Summer

'Why was she crying?' asked Jane.
'Isn't it obvious,' said Margaret.' The whole thing was a total
male ego trip from start to finish. Male aggression, male
confrontation and male compromise.'
'But you took a hand in negotiations,' said Jane.
'Sure, sure,' said Margaret impatiently.' I fully admit that. It
just shows how, despite the advantages of my background, I
needed my consciousness raised almost as much as those men.
Sharon was the only one to see through the whole patriarchal
sham.'
'That's what she said, was it?'
'Well, no, not in so many words. But I could tell. Or rather,
can tell now, with hindsight.'
'That's handy.' Jane pressed the button of the editing desk and
ran the sequence she had been editing for Margaret's
documentary on Punk. It was a rough assembly at the moment
featuring interviews with a group of very young looking kids
outside the Rainbow in Finsbury Park after a concert headlined
by the Clash, and featuring several other up and coming groups
that Margaret's researcher had alerted her to. Margaret was
surrounded by faces full of safety pins and hidden behind very
dark glasses. She was talking to one particularly sweaty boy
who seemed not be wearing any identifiable uniform nor to be
affecting the all purpose working class snarl all the others had
adopted.
'So tell me, why do you like the Clash so much?' she asked
him.
'I don't really. I mean, they're all right I suppose, but I was
mostly here for the Buzzcocks.'
Margaret turned to her camera man.

223

'Still running?' He nodded. She paused, then turned again.
'OK. So tell me, what especially appeals to you about this
group. . . The Buzz … cocks?' Her voice skidded on the name
like a pair of tongs on an ice cube.
 'I don't know really. They just make you want to dance.'
 'Don't you call it pogoing?' prompted Margaret.
 'Sometimes.' The boy went on. 'They've also got clever words,
and they were one of the groups that inspired us to do this.' He
held up a cardboard box, opened the lid and took out a record,
which he handed to Margaret. Juggling with the microphone,
she took it out of its sleeve and read the label.
 'Reject Romance' by the Twirps?' Margaret burst out
laughing. The other punks jostling for screen space in front of
the camera grew indignant.
 'Don't laugh. It's great. Peel's been playing it.' One or two
reached over and ruffled the interviewee's hair as they did so.
 Margaret managed to regain her composure.
 'And you're a Twirp, are you?'
 'Yes, and so's she.' He indicated a much more obviously punk
looking girl beside him.
 Margaret looked at the label again.
 'And you record for Wind Up Records. Or is it Wynd Up?'
 'Both, either,' said the girl. 'All three, maybe.'
 'How did they sign you up?'
 'They didn't. It's our own label,' said the boy. 'We did it
ourselves.'
 'And that's where the film ran out,' said Margaret leaning back
in her seat beside Jane's at the editing desk.' They had to go any
way, but we've fixed another interview with them tomorrow so
they can tell us all about their do-it-yourself approach.'
 Jane was silent for a moment,
 'Did the boy say what his name was?'
 Margaret laughed,

'He absolutely insisted that his name was Tommy Twirp. I expect we'll manage to prise out the truth tomorrow.'

Jane hoped and feared that that might be true. She didn't say to Margaret that the boy looked like John. Not a lot to go on.

'It's a boy.'

That's all they told her in the hospital. She hadn't wanted even to see it, for fear of changing her mind. So the baby would now be about thirteen and could look a little like John. Or herself. Maybe it did too. But then Margaret would have noticed. Trust Margaret to find her thirteen-year old son for her.

Maybe if she kept mum (she winced at the pun) no one would notice and the matter would resolve itself. She had no maternal feelings now, any more than she had had filial feelings for the poor Daventrys, shot dead in Jerusalem when she was tiny. Dead and buried, living and buried. All the same thing really. And it probably wasn't him anyway. Keep mum, yes that was the answer. Far less trouble that way.

' … next Thursday, OK?,' Margaret's voice brought her back to the present.

Jane gave a start.

'Oh, yes, fine. Good luck.'

Margaret was gone leaving a rustling of celluloid among the rushes hanging in the bin. Jane ran the Round House interview again, and tried to remember what had seemed so vitally important about getting rid of this person sight unseen.

John had tried his utmost to prevent her. Pleading with her to think about it again and again over the nine months. Towards the end she had stopped him coming to see her. Forbidden him to write, torn up his letters when he did. 'It' had arrived conveniently during the summer break, after which she had returned in October slimmer and sadder. Once delivery had been effected John's letters had stopped and she had not heard from him again directly. The grapevine would occasionally have news of his progress, if that was the word, but they moved

225

in different circles. She saw his name occasionally under articles summarising the current state of rock music for various glossy magazines with a readership avid for readymade opinion without the necessity for thought. She had even very occasionally edited interviews with him and had taken note of his changing or rather unchanging appearance with a wry smile. She had known he was out there, alive, but there seemed no very pressing reason to seek him out.

***

In a room about three miles away from Jane's cutting room, John sat listening to the latest clutch of singles he had bought from Rough Trade that afternoon. As well as the big names he had managed to get hold of an intriguingly awful sounding record he had heard on Peel the previous evening by The Twirps. He was playing it now, for the fourth or fifth time that day and was beginning to be able to make out one or two of the words. What particularly amused him was that after the song had finished there was a hoarse cry of,
  'Don't be slow, have a go!'
 On impulse John picked up the phone and dialled. He got through to the Radio One offices and managed to obtain a contact number for Wind Up records.
When he phoned that number, someone answered. It was a young boy. In his early teens, maybe. He sounded just like Jane.

Lightning Source UK Ltd.
Milton Keynes UK
27 July 2010

157454UK00001B/78/P